STAR OF LIGHT

STAR
OF LIGHT

PATRICIA M. ST. JOHN

Illustrated by Jo Anne Brubaker

MOODY PRESS
CHICAGO

By the same Author:

THE TANGLEWOODS' SECRET
TREASURES OF THE SNOW

This book was first published (1953) in England by the
Children's Special Service Mission and the Scripture
Union. All rights reserved.

ISBN 0-8024-0004-3

43 45 47 49 50 48 46 44 42

Moody Press, a ministry of the Moody Bible Institute, is
designed for education, evangelization and edification.
If we may assist you in knowing more about Christ and
the Christian life, please write us without obligation to:
Moody Press, c/o MLM, Chicago, Illinois 60610.

Printed in the United States of America

CONTENTS

INTRODUCTORY NOTE

I F YOU LOOK at a map of North Africa, you will see that at the northwest corner the waters of the Mediterranean mingle with the wild tides of the Atlantic. The great Atlantic beaches stretch for miles and miles, with the waves crashing and thundering on vast tracts of unbroken sand. Occasionally a seawall has been built with a little town sheltering behind it, but for the most part it is a lonely shore rising into sand dunes and backed by mountains.

These mountains reach right back as far as the Mediterranean coast and run in a mighty range overlooking those still blue waters. Very high are some of these mountains, snowcapped until early summer, clothed with pine trees and stunted junipers; others are merely high grassy hills, or bare rocky peaks, flanked by orchards and olive trees; and among the olive trees squat the villages—clumps of mud-thatched huts, with a well in the center and a prickly pear hedge to mark the boundaries.

PART ONE

CHAPTER ONE

Kinza—"Treasure"

A LITTLE GIRL came running down the side of the mountain one noon in spring. Gathering her cotton dress round her knees, she skipped as lightly as a lamb on her bare brown feet, leaping over drifts of wild marigold. In the water meadows below her the plum blossom was out, and from the hilltop above it looked like a sea of white foam along the riverbanks.

11

Baby goats skipped among the flowers, and the storks
had begun to build on top of the roofs. Everything
was busy and bright. The children all over the mountain stirred to the mood of spring, and leaped and
shouted and ran.

Rahma, who had taken a short cut across the hillside, reached the path with a bound, and went on
dancing down it. She was seven years old, small because she seldom had enough to eat. Her stepfather
and the elder wife disliked her, and sometimes beat
her. Her clothes were very ragged, and she worked
as hard as the mother of a family might work; yet all
her troubles could not dim the radiance of her joy
when a treat occasionally came her way—and today,
well, of today we shall see. She was to look after the
goats alone while her brother went on some myste-
rious expedition with their mother.

Free and alone for two whole hours with no other
company but the storks and the goats—two whole
hours to play in the sunshine with the kids, and no
one would scold her, or make her grind the millstone,
or carry heavy buckets of water. Her tired body,
released, felt as light as a wisp of cloud, and the marigolds and the sparkling river and the sunshine seemed
to build up a golden world about her. On it no dreary
future could cast a shadow.

She spied her brother from afar, rounding up a
couple of mischievous young kids who were trying to
get into a patch of young wheat. Spring was making

them feel crazy, and they skipped in every direction
except the right one, giving merry little bleats and
leaping high in the air. Hamid, their keeper, did not
mind at all, for he felt exactly as they did. At the mar-
gin of the field of young wheat the three of them
pranced together. Rahma came bounding in among
them, her smooth dark hair blown in wisps about her
face, her black eyes very bright.

Laughing and shouting together, they steered the
kids on to the open hillside where the rest of the flock
was scattered. Then Hamid turned, surprised, to look
at his happy little sister. He had not often seen her
so gay and free, for country girls are taught to walk
sedately and to listen to their elders and superiors.
Besides, Rahma was seven years old, and almost a
little woman.

"What have you come for?" he asked.

"To look after the goats—Mother wants you."

"Why?"

"I don't know—she wants you to go somewhere.
She has been crying and looking at little sister. I think
perhaps little sister is ill."

Her sparkling eyes clouded as she remembered her
mother's tears, for she loved her mother—only the
sunshine and freedom had made her forget all about
them. Besides, her mother often wept when no one
but Rahma was with her, so Rahma was almost used
to it.

"All right," said Hamid, "but take good care of the

goats; here's a stick for you," and he turned away and climbed the valley between the two green arms of the mountains. He walked fast because he did not want to keep his mother waiting, but he did not skip or look about him as Rahma had done, for his mind was full of wondering.

Why did his mother look so worried these days, as though she were carrying some secret load of fear? And why was she always hiding away his baby sister, keeping her out of sight whenever she heard her husband or the older wife approaching? Of course, neither of them had ever particularly liked baby sister, but they knew she was there, so why hide her? Mother even seemed afraid of him and Rahma playing with their baby nowadays. She would drive them away, and retreat into a corner of the room, her little daughter clasped against her, and always that fear in her eyes—was it evil spirits she feared? or poison? Hamid did not know, but perhaps today his mother would tell him. He walked faster.

He sighed as he climbed the hill, because until a few months ago his mother had never looked frightened. He and Rahma had never been knocked about or considered in the way. They had lived with their mother and with their own father, who loved them, in a little thatched home down the valley; there had been three other brown tousled-headed children younger than Rahma, but they had started coughing and grown thin. When the snow fell, and fuel and bread were scarce, they grew weaker and died within a few weeks of each other. Their little bodies were buried on the eastern slope of the mountain facing the sunrise, and marigolds and daisies sprang up on their graves.

Their father coughed that winter too, but no one took any notice, because, after all, a man must earn his living; so he went on working, and ploughed his spring fields, and sowed his grain. Then he came home one night and said he could work no more. Until the following autumn he lay on the rush mat and grew weaker. Zohra, his wife, and Hamid and Rahma gathered in the ripened corn, and gleaned what they could in order to buy him food, but it was no use. Then he died, leaving his wife, still young and beautiful, a penniless widow with two little children.

They sold the house and the goat and the hens and the patch of corn, and went to live with the grandmother, until, a few months later, little sister was born, bringing fresh hope and sunshine to the stricken little family. They called her Kinza, which means "treasure," and never was a baby more loved or fondled; yet, strange to say, the wee thing never played or clapped her hands like other babies. She slept a great deal, and often seemed to lie staring at nothing. Hamid sometimes wondered why the bunches of bright flowers he picked for her seemed to give her no pleasure.

When Kinza was a few months old there came a

fresh offer of marriage for their mother, and she accepted at once, because she had no work and no more money to buy bread for her two children; and the family moved to their new home.

It was not a very happy home. Si Mohamed, the husband, was already married to an older wife, but she had never had any children, so he wanted another. He did not mind taking Hamid too, because a boy of nine would be useful in looking after the goats; nor did he object to Rahma, because a girl of seven can be a useful little slave about the house; but he could not see that a baby was the slightest use to any of them, and wished to give Kinza away.

"Many childless women will be glad of a girl," he said; "and why should I bring up another man's baby!"

But young Zohra had burst into weeping and refused to do any work until he changed his mind, so he rather sullenly agreed to let Kinza stay for a time. No more was said about it—unless perhaps something had been said during the past few weeks, something that Hamid and Rahma had not heard; could that be why their mother held Kinza so close, and looked so frightened?

A voice above him called to him to run, and he looked up. His mother was standing under an old twisted olive tree that flung its shade over a well. She carried two buckets in her hand, but she had not filled them, and baby Kinza was tied on her back with a cloth. She seemed in a great hurry about something.

"Come quick, Hamid," she said impatiently. "How slowly you come up the path! Hide the buckets in the bushes—I only brought them as an excuse to leave the house, in case Fatima should want to know why I was going. Now, come with me."

"Where to, Mother?" asked the little boy, very surprised.

"Wait till we get round the corner of the mountain," replied his mother, leading the way up the steep, green grass, and walking very fast. "People will see us from the well, and will tell Fatima where we have gone. Follow quickly. I'll soon tell you."

They hurried on until they had turned the corner of the arm of the mountain and were hidden from the village, and were overlooking another valley. The young mother sat down, unhitched her cloth, and laid her baby in her lap.

"Look well at her, Hamid," she said. "Play with her and show her the flowers."

Hamid, wondering, stared long and earnestly into the strangely old, patient face of his little sister, but she did not stare back or return his smile. She seemed to be looking at something very far away, and not to see him at all. With a sudden thrill of fear he flicked his hand in front of her eyes, but she neither moved nor blinked.

"She's blind," he whispered at last. His lips felt dry, and his face was rather white.

His mother nodded, and rose quickly to her feet. "Yes," she replied, "she's blind. I've known it for some time, but I've kept it from Fatima and my husband because when they know they will probably take her away from me—why should they be bothered with another man's blind child? She can never work, and she will never marry . . ."

Her voice broke, and, blinded by her tears, she stumbled a little on the rough track. Hamid caught her arm.

"Where are we going, Mother?" he inquired again.

"To the Saint's tomb," answered his mother, hurrying on, "up behind the next hill. They say he is a very powerful saint and has healed many, but Fatima has never before given me the chance to go. Now she thinks I'm drawing water, and we must return with the buckets full. I wanted you to come with me, because it's a lonely path and I was afraid to go by myself."

They climbed in silence, too breathless to talk any more. Here, hollowed from a boulder, was a small cave shaded by a bush. The bush was festooned with dirty little screws of paper tied to its branches, and every little screw carried its tale of sorrow; the sick, the broken-hearted, the childless, the unloved, all brought their burdens to the bones of this dead man, and they all went home unhealed and uncomforted.

They laid little sister at the mouth of the cave, and

the mother bowed down and lifted herself up again, calling on the name of a God about whom she knew nothing, and on the prophet Mahomet. It was her last hope. But as she prayed a cloud passed across the sun, and a cold shadow fell on the baby. She shivered and began to cry, and groped for her mother's arms. The woman gazed eagerly into her daughter's face for a moment, and then picked her up with a disappointed sigh. God had not listened, for Kinza was still blind.

Hamid rose from the patch of marigolds on which he had been squatting, and he and his mother almost ran down the hill. They were late, and already the sun was setting behind the mountains. The storks flew past with their rattling cry, black against the rosy west, and Hamid, rebellious and bitterly disappointed, scowled at the world which was bathed in the last glow of that beautiful light.

Radiance of marigolds, tenderness of young green wheat, brightness of sunset skies—what was the good of them all? Little sister would never see them; God apparently did not care, and the dead saint would do nothing to help. Perhaps baby girls were beneath His notice.

They reached the well in silence, and Hamid drew the water for his mother, gave her the buckets, and dashed off down the valley to collect Rahma and the goats. He met them half way up the hill, for Rahma was afraid of the lengthening shadows and wanted to

go home. She slipped her small hand into his; and
the goats, who also wanted to go home, huddled
against their legs.

"Where did you go?" asked Rahma.

"To the saint's tomb," answered Hamid. "Rahma,
little sister is blind. Her eyes see nothing but darkness
—that's why Mother hides her away. She does not
want Fatima and Si Mohamed to know."

Rahma stood still, horrified. "Blind?" she echoed—
and then, as the thought struck her, she added
quickly, "and the saint—couldn't he make her see?"

Hamid shook his head. "I don't think that saint is
much good," he said rather boldly. "Mother went
there before when Father coughed, but nothing happened—Father died."

"It is the will of God," said Rahma, and she
shrugged her shoulders and spread out her hands with
a hopeless little gesture, as much as to say, "There is
nothing more we can do about it!" Then, clinging
close together, because night was falling, they
climbed the hill, and the goats' eyes gleamed like
green lanterns in the dusk.

"I hate the dark," whispered Rahma with a little
shiver. But Hamid stared up into the sky, deep blue
through a filigree of olive leaves.

"I love the stars," he said.

CHAPTER TWO

The Discovery

THEY REACHED the village ten minutes later, and passed by dark huts. Through open doors glowing charcoal gleamed cheerfully in clay pots, and families squatted round their evening meal by dim lamplight. But at some little distance from their own house they could hear the angry voice of Fatima, the older wife, scolding their mother.

Fatima hated the new wife and her three children, and made life as hard as she could for them in every possible way. She was bowed and withered by long years of drudgery, and Zohra was still young and beautiful. Fatima had longed in vain for a baby, while Zohra had had six, so perhaps it was small wonder that the older woman was so jealous, and had been so angry at their coming. She vented her hatred by sitting cross-legged on the mattress like a queen all day, and making Zohra and Rahma work like slaves. Zohra had only escaped to the well because Fatima had fallen asleep—and unfortunately she had not slept long. Furious at the young woman's absence, she had sent a neighboring child to the top of the hill to spy out her whereabouts—so Zohra, carrying her buckets, had arrived home to find that Fatima knew all about her expedition.

"Wicked, deceitful, lazy one!" shouted Fatima. "You can't deceive me. Give me that child! let me see for myself why you hide her away, and hold her so secretly, and creep with her to the tomb—give me her, I say. I insist on having her."

She snatched the baby roughly from Zohra's grasp, and carried her to the light, and the mother with a resigned gesture of despair let her empty arms fall to her side. After all, Fatima must know soon. They could not hide it much longer, and she had better find out for herself.

The frightened children squatted in the shadows by

the wall, their dark eyes very big. The hut was perfectly silent as Fatima passed her hands over the baby limbs, and stared into Kinza's still face. Hamid, holding his breath, was conscious of little sounds he had never noticed before—the slow, rhythmical munching of the ox in the stall; the rustle of straw as the kids nuzzled against their mothers; the subdued crooning of roosted hens.

Then the silence was broken by a triumphant cackle of laughter from the old woman, and Kinza, whose ears were acutely sensitive to loud noises and angry voices, gave a frightened cry. Fatima picked her up and almost flung her back into her mother's lap.

"Blind," she announced—"blind as night!—and you knew—you knew all the time! You brought her here to your husband's house to be a burden on us all forever—never to work, never to marry—and you hid her away lest we should know. Oh, most deceitful of women! our husband shall know about this tonight. Now up and prepare his supper, and you, Rahma, blow up the charcoal. When he has eaten his food we shall hear what he has to say."

The frightened little girl sprang up and set to work with the bellows till the flames leaped from the glowing charcoal and flung strange shadows on the walls. Zohra, trembling, laid her baby in the swinging wooden cradle that hung from a beam, and set to work to mash the beans and beat in the oil, for her

husband had gone to speak to a neighbor, and would
be in any time now. They were only just ready when
they heard his firm steps coming along the path, and
a moment later he appeared in the doorway, a tall
man, black-eyed and black-bearded, with a hard,
cruel mouth. He wore a long garment of dark homespun goat's wool, with a white turban wound round
his head. He did not speak to his wives or to his step-
children, but sat down cross-legged in front of the
low, round table and motioned for the food to be set
before him. If he noticed Fatima's triumph, and the
white, scared faces of Zohra and the children, he said
nothing.

Zohra set the hot dish in the center of the table and
the silent family gathered round. There were no
spoons, but she broke two large pieces of bread for
her husband and Fatima and three small pieces for
herself, Hamid, and Rahma.

"In the name of God," they murmured as they
scooped their bread in the center dish, for these words
would drive away evil spirits who might be lurking
round the table. Sometimes at midday when the sun
was shining Rahma forgot to say them, but she never
forgot at night, for the flickering shadows and dark
corners made her feel afraid; evil spirits seemed very
real and near after the lamps had been lit. And certainly tonight the little home was full of evil spirits—
dark spirits of jealousy and anger and hatred and
cruelty and fear. Even little Kinza in her hanging

cradle seemed to feel the atmosphere, and wailed fretfully. Si Mohamed frowned.

"Stop that noise," he growled. "Pick her up."

The mother obeyed, and sat down again with her baby held very close against her breast. Fatima waited a moment until her husband had finished eating, then she held out her arms.

"Give that child to me," she said threateningly, and Zohra handed over her baby and burst into tears.

"What is the matter?" asked Si Mohamed irritably. His wives might quarrel all they pleased—wives always did quarrel—but he disliked them doing it in front of him. He had been ploughing all day, and was tired.

"Yes, what is the matter indeed!" sneered Fatima, and she held out the baby at arm's length so that the lamplight suddenly shone straight on to her face. But she neither screwed up her eyes nor turned from it. Si Mohamed stared at her fixedly.

"Blind!" cried Fatima, as she had shouted before. "Blind, blind, blind! and Zohra knew it—she has deceived us all."

"I didn't," sobbed Zohra, rocking to and fro.

"You did," shouted the old woman.

"Silence, you women," said their husband sternly, and the quarrel ceased instantly. Once again there was dead silence in the dim hut. Rahma suddenly felt cold with fear, and crept closer to the dying charcoal. Her stepfather scrutinized the tiny face—flashed the

light in front of it—jerked his hands toward it, until
he was satisfied that the old woman spoke the truth.

"Truly," he agreed, "she is blind."

But the dreaded outburst of rage never came. He
handed Kinza back to her mother, half closed his
eyes, and lit a long thin pipe. He sat puffing away in
silence for some time, until the hut was filled with
sickly fumes, and then he said,

"Blind children can be very profitable—keep that
baby carefully. She may bring us much money."

"How?" asked Zohra nervously, her arms tightening
on her baby.

"By begging," replied her husband. "Of course, we
cannot take her begging ourselves, for I am a very
honorable man; but there are beggars who would be
glad to hire her to sit with them in the markets;
people are sorry for blind children, and give liberally.
I believe I know of one who would pay to borrow her
when she is a little older."

Zohra said nothing—she dared not; but Hamid and
Rahma gave each other a long rebellious look across
the table. They knew the beggar of whom their father
spoke—an old man dressed in filthy, ancient rags, who
swore horrible oaths. They did not want their precious Kinza to go to that old man. He would certainly
ill-treat her and frighten her.

Their father saw the look through half-closed eyelids. He clapped his hands sharply.

"To bed, you children," he ordered, "quick!"

They rose hurriedly, mumbled good night, and scuttled into dark corners of the room. There were low mattresses laid along the wall; curling themselves up on these, they pulled strips of blanket over them, and fell fast asleep. They neither undressed nor washed nor said their prayers; indeed, if anyone had suggested they should do so, they would probably have thought it very foolish.

Hamid never knew why he woke that night, for he usually slept soundly till sunrise; but about two in the morning he suddenly sat up in bed, wide awake. A patch of bright moonlight was shining through the window on to Kinza's cradle, and the wee girl was moaning and stirring in her sleep.

Hamid slipped from his mattress, and stood beside her in that beautiful island of silver light. The rest of the family were all deeply asleep in the shadows, their quarrels and sorrows forgotten and soothed. Hamid rocked the crib, and stroked his baby sister's dark head until her puckered face grew peaceful. She lay at rest with one tiny hand stretched out appealingly on the cover.

Hamid watched her somberly, and suddenly a great wave of protective tenderness seemed to come sweeping over him. She was so small, so patient, and so defenseless. Well, he would see to it that no harm came to her. All his life he would guide her through her darkness, and protect her with his love—he would be her refuge and her light. His heart swelled for a moment, and then he remembered with a throb of pain that he was only a little boy himself and completely in his stepfather's hand. They might take Kinza away from him, and then his love would be powerless to reach her.

Was there no stronger love to shelter her, no more certain light to lead her? He did not know. Very softly he stooped to kiss her, and then tiptoed back to bed. And Kinza, in her moonlit cradle, smiled a little, tucked two fingers into her mouth, and slept as peacefully as a baby princess in a palace.

CHAPTER THREE

Si Mohamed's Plans

BLIND KINZA sat in the doorway of her hut and lifted her small face to the sunshine. It was Thursday, and on Thursday Kinza went to work. She was two-and-a-half years old now, and quite old enough, in her father's opinion, to earn her living like the rest of them.

She sat still and patient, her weak legs folded under

29

her, her hands clasped quietly in her lap. It was quite early, and Hamid, who carried her to her job, had taken the cow to pasture and would not be back for half an hour or so. In the meantime she was free to enjoy herself, and Kinza enjoyed herself quite a lot in her own way.

She had never seen the sun rise up behind the mountain, but she knew that, if about this time every morning she sat just outside her doorway, a tender warmth would suddenly stream over her, bathing her body in comfort and delight. At the first touch of its rays on her lifted expectant face she would laugh for joy, and hold out her arms as though to a loved friend. Then she would fold her hands in her lap again, and sit deeply content until it became too hot. In her short life she had known a good deal of jostling and slapping, of rough pushing away by those who did not want her, but the sun always touched her gently and so she loved it.

As long as the sun shone and the weather was fine she was, on the whole, a happy little child. Never having seen the light she could not miss it, and there were many good things to feel. There was the warmth and shelter of her mother's lap, the clasp of her brother's strong arms, and the wet noses of kids nuzzled into her hands. There was the touch of the sun on her body and the wind on her face. Sometimes she was allowed to sit by her mother as she sorted the corn, and Kinza would pick up handfuls of warm husks and let them slip through her fingers. That was one of her greatest treats.

There were lovely things to hear, too—the bleating and clucking and lowing of the inhabitants of the little farm, and the muffled sound of the millstone which meant that her mother was not far away; the cheerful clatter of buckets that heralded the arrival of Rahma from the well, the puffing of the bellows and roaring of charcoal that suggested something to eat in the near future. Best of all was the patter of homing goats, because behind the goats came Hamid, and to Kinza, Hamid was the most wonderful person in the world.

She knew all her family's footsteps, and she knew now that Hamid was coming toward her, from the particular sound of his bare feet on the dry mud. She held up her arms and gave a delighted squeak. Hamid picked her up and tied her firmly on his back.

"Market day, little sister," he announced. "Have you had some breakfast?"

Kinza nodded. Half an hour ago she had drunk a bowlful of sweet black coffee and eaten a hunk of brown bread. It was the best breakfast she knew, and she had enjoyed it immensely.

"Come then," said Hamid, and they set off together, keeping under the olives to begin with, because by nine o'clock in the summer the sun was blazing hot. But very soon they left the olive trees behind them, and the path to market ran between wheat fields ripe

for harvest; every stalk was bowed with heavy gold,
and the air was drowsy with the smell of poppies.
Kinza, who could go to sleep whenever and wherever
she pleased, laid her head down on her brother's
shoulder and shut her eyes, lulled by the sound of the
wind rustling over the corn. The cows were feeling
sleepy, too; they stood knee-deep in the muddy shallows of the river, with the flies buzzing round their
heads.

There were many people on the path that morning,
for on Thursday, instead of the village going to the
market, the market came to the village. Each of the
larger villages had its own special day when all who
had anything to sell traveled over the mountains and
squatted on their particular market place—which is
why the name of Hamid's village meant Thursday.
Several times on their journey Hamid backed into the
corn to make way for some stately merchant riding
along on horseback, with his wife, bowed down under some heavy burden, panting along behind him.

As they reached the market place the crowds became thicker. It was an area of burnt yellow grass,
shaded by eucalyptus trees, and the sellers sat cross-
legged on the ground, with their wares piled up in
front of them, while the buyers stampeded round
them. Kinza hated it. She hated the jostling and jolting and noise; she hated the dust that made her
sneeze, and the flies that crawled over her face, and
the fleas that bit her legs. Most of all she hated the

moment when Hamid deserted her and left her to the care of the old beggar.

But Hamid, in order to ease the pain of parting, had contrived a plan. If during the week he could beg, borrow, or steal a gourda (which is a coin worth about one-fourth of a cent), he would save it until Thursday morning, and as they crossed the market he would exchange it proudly for a lump of sticky green candy, studded with nuts. And licking that green candy was the biggest treat Kinza knew.

Hamid, very much at home in the market, steered his way deftly through the crowds, elbowing, ducking, and dodging until he reached the patch of sand where Kinza and the old beggar sat side by side. He made a point of arriving before the beggar because that gave him time to settle Kinza on the sand to eat the green candy. Hamid took a few secret licks himself first, and then handed it over, warm and wet, to his sister. She clasped it in her right hand, loving its sweet stickiness, and began to lick it all over, going round and round with the tip of her little pink tongue. In her left hand she clutched the hem of Hamid's tunic tightly, lest the roaring crowd should sweep him away from her.

They had not been there long before the old beggar came shuffling toward them, with a colored drum in his hand. He was amazingly dirty and old, and his coat looked like a patchwork quilt falling to pieces. Hamid kissed his hand politely and received the coin that was paid to his father weekly for the loan of Kinza. But, instead of dismissing him curtly as he usually did, the old beggar spoke to him.

"When your father comes down to buy," he growled, "tell him I have business with him."

Hamid nodded, freed himself gently from Kinza's grasp, and made off; and Kinza, finding herself bereft, had a quiet little weep, until the old beggar noticed and slapped her for it. Then she sniffed, pulled herself together, and work began.

Her work was not very difficult during the early part of the day. All she had to do was to sit with her small face lifted to the light so that all could see she was blind, and hold out her hand. The old beggar sat beside her, thumping his drum to make people look at her, and chanting and swaying. Quite a number felt sorry for the tiny white-faced child, and gave her coins which she handed to her master. So they sat until noon, and the sun rose higher, and the dust and the flies grew thicker. The crowd milled round them and the stray dogs sniffed them. Once or twice somebody failed to see her at all, and tripped right over her. It was all exciting.

At noon Kinza's master gave her a piece of dark rye bread and a cup of water, and because she had collected quite a lot of money during the morning he gave her a squashed plum. It was delicious. She sucked all her ten fingers in turn, lest she should lose one drop of the juice.

The afternoon was harder than the morning, for by two o'clock Kinza began to grow sleepy. Her dark head, tied up in its cotton cloth, began to nod heavily, and her eyes just would not keep open. She longed for her mother's lap, so all unnoticed she nestled against the old man's rags and found a place of rest for her weary head.

But only for a few minutes. He saw what had happened, and jerked her angrily upright. All bewildered, she rubbed her knuckles in her eyes, stretched herself, and tumbled forward. Once again he jerked her back, slapped her, and propped her up against him, and thus with her outstretched hand supported by the other she sat begging, half-asleep, dreaming no doubt of beautiful baby secrets, until the beggar suddenly got up in a hurry, and she fell over sideways.

He sat her up with an impatient bump. "Bad child!" he growled, "sit and beg till I come back."

He had risen because, on the outskirts of the crowd, he had seen the tall figure of Kinza's stepfather looking about for him. The farmer would not wish to speak to the beggar in the open market, so they withdrew together behind a huge eucalyptus tree and stood talking.

"You wanted me?" asked the farmer.

"Yes," said the old beggar. "I'm leaving the village. The country people are growing greedy and irreligious, and give little to honorable beggars, so I'm going to the great town on the coast—I and my wife.

The great feast will soon be here, and they say beggars grow rich in the streets of the town. Now this is what I want to say—Give me that blind child of yours. You are not one of the noble profession of beggars, and you can never make use of her, but she brings me great gain. My wife will look after her, and I will pay you a good sum for her."

Kinza's stepfather hesitated. He knew that he was plotting a very wicked thing, but he needed money badly. His cow had strayed into a neighbor's corn and had been put in the cows' prison. It could only be redeemed at a high price. His harvest was poor this year, and Kinza, while she earned a little, was and always would be an extra mouth to feed.

Some faint feeling that might once have been a conscience stirred in him, but he refused to listen to it. After all, Kinza was not his child. Hamid was eleven, almost a man, and could soon be turned adrift to earn his own living, and Rahma could be married off in three or four years. But this might be the first and last chance he would ever have of getting rid of Kinza.

"How much will you give me?" he said at last.

The beggar mentioned a small sum. The farmer fell into a towering rage at such meanness, and mentioned a very large sum. The beggar fell into a towering rage at such covetousness, but stated his price a little higher, while the farmer consented to come a little lower. Thus the bargaining went on. You would have thought they were about to murder each other, but the passers-by hardly turned their heads. For that is the way prices are fixed in the country, and the final sum was exactly halfway between what both had asked in the first place.

"Right," said the beggar at last. "I'll be leaving the village at dawn on the first day of the week. When you hand over the child I will hand over the money, and it shall be done in the presence of witnesses."

Though neither showed it, both were pleased. The old beggar fought his way back to his newly purchased property, hoping she had managed to collect some coins during his absence. But his newly purchased property had done nothing of the sort. She had crept into a patch of dappled sun and shade and lay fast asleep, curled up in a ball like a tired kitten.

CHAPTER FOUR

A Secret Meeting

HAMID STOOD on the outskirts of the market, his thin brown face upturned, and his eyes glued to the top of the mosque, waiting for the priest to appear and shout the four o'clock prayer call. That call sounded the hour of Kinza's release, when he might carry her off, safe for another week.

The crowd was thinning now, and Hamid caught oc-

casional glimpses of his baby sister sitting in a dejected
little heap beside her master. She was in disgrace for
having fallen asleep, and her weary attitude made
Hamid impatient to rescue her. He stood first on one
bare foot and then on the other. Then he stood on
both and wriggled his toes in the hot sand, but he
never moved his bright, dark eyes from the top of the
mosque.

The mosque was the village temple—a building
with a square tower dazzling white against the burning blue. From its summit rose a gleaming golden
crescent, and, as Hamid stood watching, the old priest
appeared, bearded and majestic in his robes of office,
and sent his chanted prayer call ringing across the
market to the village beyond:

"There is one God," he cried, "and Mahomet is his
prophet." Faithful Moslems flocked to the temple to
recite their prayer. Others took off their shoes and
prayed where they stood, facing east, bowing low,
and sometimes kneeling with their foreheads on the
ground. To them it was a prayer call, but to Hamid it
was the call of Kinza's release. The instant he caught
sight of the priest he scudded across the market,
kissed the old beggar's hand in greeting, and snatched
up his little sister.

He had brought her a leathery ring of fried dough;
she clutched it eagerly and took a mouthful. In the
joy of feeling his arms safe about her once more she
forgot all the hunger and thirst and weariness of that

long day, and nestled her downy head into his neck, crooning with delight. Her tired muscles and stiff back relaxed. She dribbled as she ate her mouthful of doughnut, tucked the rest of it down her dress, and went fast asleep, as she had been longing to do for the past three hours. Hamid, a little bowed by the dead weight of her, wandered home along the river path in the sweltering heat.

It was so hot that he sat down to rest under a fig tree and watched the lazy cows in the shallows of the river. A few women were washing their clothes just above where the cows stood, rubbing their white garments on stones. Very soon the figs would be ripe, and oleanders would bloom along the river banks. Half drowsily he began thinking about the river. Where did it go when it left his valley and flowed out into a strange world where he had never been? One day he would go and see—he would go when the oleanders were out, and follow their pink, winding tracks all the way to the great ocean.

He sat dozing under the fig tree until the sun drew near to the mountain top, bathing the world with that strange last light that seems both to silence and illumine the world. The wheat fields had ceased to rustle, and the cows had stopped munching. Everything seemed to hold its breath and wait for sunset, and the little boy hurried up the hill on his brown toes, making no sound.

Once again, as night fell, the family gathered round the clay bowl and ate their supper by firelight and candlelight. Kinza woke up, refreshed by her sleep, and sat on her mother's knees, flushed and bright-eyed, opening her mouth for food like a hungry baby bird. Hamid watched her, loving her, and remembering the pressure of her weary little body against his back—always, always, he would protect her and make her happy.

The cows munched in the shed, and an old dog with a torn ear wandered in and lay down with his head on Rahma's lap. Moths and bats fluttered in and out, and the cat crept up and stuck her head into the clay pot to have supper with the family. Twice they pushed her away, but she was very persistent so in the end they let her be. After all, there was plenty for everyone.

A tiny wind breathed into the doorway, sweet with the smell of herbs which grew in boxes outside the hut. Hamid, tired by his climb, lay down to sleep, and in his dreams the old beggar seemed to get bigger and bigger, till somehow he stood, enormous and terrifying, between him and Kinza . . . He woke suddenly to find that the moon had risen and the grown-ups were still sitting talking round the dead charcoal.

It must have been some new quality of fear or urgency in his mother's voice that woke him, for they were not talking loudly. In the silver beams he could see their faces clearly—his father grim and determined, Fatima cruelly pleased, his mother pale and pleading.

"It is the only offer we shall ever get for her," said Si Mohamed doggedly. "She will be provided for for life."

"Life!" cried the mother bitterly, "there will be no life! She will die—she is so little and so weak. . . ."

"A blind child is better dead!" remarked Fatima.

The mother turned angrily on the old woman, but the father silenced them both by raising his hand.

"Silence, you foolish women!" he ordered. "Let there be no more talk about this. The child must come with me three days from now at dawn."

He rose majestically, and Fatima rose too; but Zohra stayed crouched by the dead fire, rocking herself to and fro in the moonlight.

"Little daughter! little daughter!" she murmured brokenly to herself, and Hamid lay quite still and watched her. He dared not speak or go to her for fear of waking his stepfather. But his hot little heart beat very fast, and his mind was resolutely made up.

"It shall not be!" he said to himself over and over again. "I will not let her go. It shall not be!"

He watched his mother creep away from the embers at last and lie down sorrowfully to sleep. He watched the patch of moonlight move across the doorway and encircle the cradle where Kinza lay dreaming. He saw the pale summer dawn begin to glimmer, and heard the first cock-crow and the cattle turn over in the stall—all the time he lay thinking, thinking, thinking. But his thinking got him nowhere, and just before daybreak he fell into a deep sleep; to be awakened two hours later by his stepfather prodding him with his foot.

"Wake up, you lazy creature!" growled Si Mohamed. "It's time you had the goats out."

Hamid rolled off his mattress, washed his face and hands in a bucket, and started to eat his breakfast. Gobbling his bread and sipping his bowl of coffee he glanced at his mother. Her face was pale, and there were dark circles under her eyes, but she did not look as unhappy as he had expected. There was a very determined expression in her face, as though she had quite made up her mind about something. Once Hamid found her staring hard at him, and he returned her gaze, steady and equally determined. She raised her eyebrows a little and he gave a slight nod. A secret understanding flashed between them. At the earliest possible opportunity they would hold council together.

They did not have to wait very long. Hamid drove out his goats and left them browsing on the hillside, well out of sight behind the prickly pear hedges. With a crust of bread saved from his breakfast he bribed a friend to keep an eye on them, and then crept back and watched through a gap in the hedge. Presently he saw his mother go across to the barn where the grindstone stood, and after a few minutes he slipped in and joined her.

Kinza was sitting as usual with her face lifted to the eastern mountain, for any moment now the sun would rise over the top of it. Hamid's mother sat cross-legged, turning the heavy wheel, and the granary smelt sweet with the fragrance of crushed corn. Hamid crouched down beside her and laid his hand on her arm.

"Mother," he whispered. "I heard last night. Is it the old beggar who is having Kinza?"

His mother turned toward him, and her calm steady gaze rested on him for a moment, as though weighing him up. He was a thin little boy, small for his age, but tough and wiry—and his love for Kinza was very strong.

"So my husband thinks," she replied, "but I say that it shall not be. I will not have Kinza starved in those cruel streets. No, Hamid, you must take her somewhere else—you can save her if you wish."

"Me!" echoed Hamid, amazed: but the look he turned on his mother was reassuring. It was full of gallant, willing courage—and there was just a trace of merriment in it, too.

CHAPTER FIVE

The Nurse's House

LISTEN," said his mother. She turned from the grind-stone, and laid her hands on his knees. In the cool half light of the granary her voice sounded strangely impressive to Hamid—like words burned into his very soul. His eyes never left her face as she spoke, and all his life he never forgot what she said to him.

"Four years ago," said the mother, "at the time of

the great pilgrimage, your father took me to the tomb across the mountains. We left you children with your grandmother, but I carried your little brother Absalom on my back, because he was only a baby. After we had visited the tomb, your father wished to go on to the town twenty miles beyond, in order to see the market and trade a little. All day we walked, from sunrise to sunset, and the sun beat down on us, and the trucks bringing the pilgrims back to the main road rattled past, almost choking us with dust. By the time we reached the town my feet were cut and blistered and Absalom was crying and feverish. His eyelids were swollen and stuck together, and he could not look at the light.

"It was a pleasant town, with fountains running in the streets. I bathed Absalom's eyes in the clean cold water. We slept at the inn yard, under the stars, and I felt rested when we woke next morning, but Absalom's eyes were still closed and swollen with the heat and dust. Your father went off to the market, but I sat holding my baby, shading his eyes from the light, and brushing the flies off him, for there were many donkeys in the yard, and the place seemed black with flies. As I sat there, a woman of the town came up and began chatting to me, and as we chatted she noticed the child.

" 'Your baby is sick?' she asked.

" 'Yes,' I replied, and turned his face toward her so that she might see.

"She got up quickly. 'Come quick,' she said; 'there's just time. I'll take you to the house of the English nurse; she'll give you good medicine and heal your baby. She healed my little boy when he rubbed prickly pear thorns into his eyes.'

"I hung back. 'I have no money,' I said.

" 'It doesn't matter,' replied the woman; 'she is a holy woman, and heals without money for love of her Saint. He is a good saint and has mercy on the poor.'

" 'But,' I objected, 'the English are rich, and live in grand houses. She will not receive me.'

" 'But she lives in one of our houses,' answered the woman; 'and those who go to her for healing are mostly poor. None are ever turned away—I tell you she receives them in the name of her Saint.'

"So I followed, much afraid, but eager for the medicine that would cure my baby's eyes. She led me down a narrow back street to a house with an open door. There were people coming out of that door— poor people like me, with babies tied on their backs. Some carried bottles of medicine and none of them looked afraid.

"We were only just in time, for the room within was nearly empty, and later on we might not have found the nurse at home. She was tall, and her hair and eyes were light. I had never seen anyone like her before. She spoke graciously to all, and I saw her take little children up in her arms as though she loved them. As I watched her, my fear went away, and when everyone else had gone I went up to her and held out Absalom. She led me to a mattress and we sat down together. She took Absalom in her lap and examined his eyes. Her hands were very gentle. He didn't even cry.

"She asked me many questions about him, and then she gave me medicine for his fever and ointment for his eyes. While she fetched them I looked at a picture on the wall. It was the picture of a Man with a kind face, holding a little child in his arms, and little children clinging to his robe, looking up at him.

"I asked her who that Man was, and she said it was one called Jesus, who was sent from God to show us the way to Heaven. She told me a lot about Him; how He healed the sick, and made blind people see, and loved all men, rich and poor, grown-ups and children. I can't remember all she said, but I know she loved the Man in the picture and wanted to be like Him—and that was why she gave medicine and was kind to Absalom."

Zohra paused, and then went on speaking very slowly.

"And I think for the sake of the Man in the picture she would shelter Kinza, and so you must carry Kinza to her. You must start tonight when the moon is full, and you must walk all night and hide by day—for Si Mohamed will certainly search for you. He need not know you have gone till tomorrow night. I will send Rahma out early with the goats before he's awake,

and tell him you have taken them. He never troubles
to look at Kinza, in any case, and I'll put a pillow in
the cradle in case Fatima glances in. By the time he
comes home from work it will be dusk, and he cannot
send out a search by night, nor will I tell him where
you've gone. By the next day you will be nearly
there."

The child's eyes were bright with fear and excitement, but he only said,

"How shall I know the way?"

"I've thought of that," replied his mother. "There
is only one road on which you can travel. If you take
the main bus road you will certainly be seen, and it is
the longest way round. The direct way through the
mountains is too lonely, and you would never find it.
But there is a third way, and that you must take. You
must follow the river to the top of the valley and then
you must climb the mountain. It is very high, but you
must just journey to the top. Below you will see another river in a valley, and if you follow the road
along the bank, you will at last reach a big main road
with traffic—cars and big trucks laden with tree-
trunks from the forests. If you start walking up this
road, it may be one of these trucks will give you a
ride, for the town lies about thirty miles along it up
the mountains. If you cannot get a ride you must walk
it, and may God help you."

"And when I get there?" breathed the boy.

"When you get there," said his mother, "you must

find the house of the English nurse. Do not ask, but just watch. She lives in a street behind the market and opposite the doorway of the inn. Her house is the last one in the street. A passage runs up the side of her house. Go to her, tell her all our story, and give her Kinza. She will know what to do next."

Hamid looked doubtful. "But what if she doesn't want Kinza?" he asked.

The mother shook her head. "She won't turn her away," she replied confidently. "She told me her Saint in the picture never turned anyone away. For the sake of her Saint I know she will receive her and be good to her. Now you must go back to your goats, and I must finish the grinding, or Fatima will be so angry. Think on what I've told you, and I'll bake extra loaves of bread for you to carry on your journey."

Hamid rose to go back to his goats, feeling like someone in a dream. The sun had risen over the mountain while they were talking, and Kinza on the step was laughing and stretching out her arms. The goats cropped the pasture, the river sparkled and the harvest fields gleamed. The world was really just the same as it had been yesterday, but to the eyes of the little boy it seemed different. His friends the mountains looked suddenly strange and menacing now that he knew he must cross them alone, and he no longer wanted to know where the river went. Yet in spite of his fear he never thought of refusing to go. Like some knight-errant of old, he had pledged his troth to his lady nearly two years ago by moonlight, and there was no turning back—not even when the lady in question was merely a skinny, toddling baby with tangled curls and eyes that had never seen light.

He whistled softly; a few young goats grazing near came up to him pushing their noses into his lap, and he suddenly knew that he loved them, and was sorry to leave them. These were the kids he had taught to walk, and carried when they were tired, and switched when they made for the young corn. He fondled their ears and stumpy horns, and wondered when he would see them again. For the first time he began to consider his own future, as well as Kinza's. He certainly could not come back for a long time. His stepfather would be much too angry.

He led them home early that evening and sat quietly down beside his mother and Rahma, who were busy spinning wool. Rahma teasled out the raw tangle on two pin-studded pieces of wood, and his mother turned the fuzzy cones on her wheel, drawing them into threads. Both were working very hard, because Fatima was sitting by watching, and neither spoke when the little boy joined them.

Yet he felt the sympathy of their silent companionship and his young heart ached. Except when his mother had gone on that five days' pilgrimage, he had never spent a night of his life away from her. Now he must leave her for a long time. He dared not speak in the presence of the old woman, but it did not matter.

The bond between mother and son is very strong the world over, and now without lifting her eyes from the humming wheel she discerned his speechless cry. Her silent love flowed out to him, comforting him, strengthening him. Rahma, who knew nothing of what was happening, broke into a very happy little chant as she tossed her wool.

The evening dragged on and the light faded. Sunset flamed in the sky, and paled again; dusk fell, and then night. The little boy sat and watched, as he had watched hundreds of times before, but tonight it was different. For the first time in his life he was not hungry when the family gathered round the supper bowl, but he forced himself to eat lest his father should notice. Then without a word he went and lay down near the door and waited, battling with his tumultuous fears and thoughts until his father should go to sleep, and the moon should rise.

He watched his father lie down at last, and listened till his breathing became heavy and regular—yes, he was sleeping deeply, snoring in his dreams. Only a little longer now. Hamid crept to the edge of the mattress, and waited with his eyes glued to the mountain. Already the crest was outlined against a circle of light.

And then it came—flooding the world so silently, bathing it in silver. Hamid lay for a moment marveling at the transfiguration. That ugly black puddle by the goatshed had been transformed into a pool of liquid light. The rusty ploughshare gleamed as though studded with jewels. The very rubbish heap under the hedge looked level and moon-kissed. On perfectly silent feet Hamid stepped through the doorway and slipped behind the granary.

The old dog cocked its ears and rattled its chain, and Hamid held his breath. If the dog should bark the whole plan would be ruined. He flung himself down beside it, burying his face in its mangy coat, fondling its ears, and speechlessly imploring it to be silent. It turned its large head and licked the child's cheek, puzzled but loyal.

So he crouched waiting, with his arms round the dog's neck, listening for his mother. The dear home scents of cattle and crushed corn wafted round him like invisible bands holding him back. But the path, a white ribbon in the moonlight, lured him on to his great adventure. He jumped as his mother, with Kinza in her arms, appeared round the granary, noiseless as a ghost.

In complete silence she bound Kinza to his back. The baby, bewildered, but perfectly trustful, laid her head down on his shoulder and went fast asleep again. Then his mother tied two loaves of bread on his other shoulder, took both his hands in hers and kissed them. He in turn pressed her fingers to his lips and clung close to her for a moment. Then she put him gently from her and stood watching as he passed out of the gate. Not a word had passed between them. Into the small grubby hands, so clinging, so passionately kissed, she had placed her dearest treasure. Of stronger hands she knew nothing.

Then, content with what she had done, she went back to her hut—to the empty cradle and the anger of her husband. And Hamid, like some small craft cut loose from its moorings and swept out into uncharted seas, set off along his silver path.

CHAPTER SIX

A Long, Hard Journey

THE PATH did not remain silver for long. It dipped into the black shadows of the olive trees, and Hamid shivered and stumbled over a root. Righting himself, he hurried on, and came out on the open, moon-washed hillside, where the grass was short and burnt. Hamid glanced up at the low pass between the hills and made toward it. On his left clustered groups of huts, straggling outposts of the village, and Hamid thought wistfully of all the children lying dreaming beside their mothers inside those dark doorways. Yet he did not feel as frightened as he had feared he would. The night was warm and sweet-scented and kind to lonely pilgrims who had to travel through it. He reached the top of the hill out of breath, and paused for a last backward look at his home.

He could see it quite clearly—a prickly pear hedge surrounding a mud yard, enclosing all that had been his world up till now; a thatched hut, a charcoal fire and a cradle; mother and the little sister; the spinning wheel, the corn sieve, the water pots and the grind-stone; a small fawn cow and a flock of goats; an old dog with torn ears—it had been a very pleasant life as long as the weather was warm and his stepfather kept out of the way. Then he went over the top of the pass, and his home was lost to view. Instead, there stretched out at his feet a strange new moonlit world and a silver road winding toward high mountains.

And then as he jogged downhill to the plain he suddenly felt afraid, for he was passing the outskirts of the village burial ground, and surely there must be evil spirits lingering in this place of death. He began to run, but remembered that he was close to those three little graves where some four years ago they had laid Absalom and Mohamed and Habeeba. Their baby spirits, at least, were not evil. He wondered where they were. Just before Absalom had died he had cried out that it was so dark, and Hamid had sat beside on the mat all day and held his hand lest he should feel lonely; till Absalom's grasp had grown weak and cold, and at last the patient little brother had realized that his hand had no more power to comfort, and Absalom was carried away. But where was the little child-spirit? was it still afraid and fluttering in the dark? Hamid did not know. Perhaps the Saint called Jesus, who took little ones in His arms, had mercy on lost children stolen away by death. He murmured the name softly to himself as a charm against all that might harm him and, still running, reached the path by the river.

Looking back later on, he remembered little about the weary hours of that first night. He arrived at the stony road by the river, and trudged the length of the plain on feet that began to feel sore and bruised. Sometimes an owl hooted from an olive tree and made him jump, but otherwise his eyes were so heavy that he seemed to be walking in a dream. Kinza, slumbering, lay like a dead weight on his back, and seemed to grow much heavier as the night passed. One thing only he noticed clearly, and that was the circling courses of the stars above him. He watched the shapes of the constellations rising from the horizon, then twinkling down on him from open heavens, then wheeling toward the further horizon. And at this point, drowsy though he was, he noticed a breath of wind and a sort of shivering in the wheat fields by the

river, as though the world were turning in its sleep
and breathing lightly. He also noticed that the ground
beneath his feet was no longer flat. He had begun
climbing.

Half an hour later, still stumbling upward, he
realized that light was stealing over the mountain.
Heavy-eyed, white-faced, footsore and cold, he
turned to look behind him. The grass was thick and
white with dew and spiders' webs, and a mist hung
like a veil over the river. But faint in the grey dawn
he could see the way he had come. The hill in front of
the village reared up dim and ghostly, and between
him and it stretched a long valley and the lower slopes
of a great mountain. He had come a good way
through the night, and since his father was unlikely
to discover his flight until evening, he was safe to
cross the peak that day. On the morrow he must hide
from sunrise to sunset.

Then the east began to flush gloriously, and
through a gap in the hills he watched the sun as it
rose, scattering the mists on the river, tinting the
water with its bright reflections. A host of hidden
birds began to twitter, and Kinza woke up. Hamid
placed her on the ground, and they sat side by side,
one watching and the other feeling.

Hamid broke two pieces off the loaf, and they
munched in silence. Then he led Kinza to a little
stream running down the side of the path, and she
drank from his cupped hands. He washed her, too,

as well as he could, for it was important that she should look attractive when they reached their unknown friend. He wished he had asked his mother for a quarter of the family comb, so that Kinza could have looked a little less like a neglected doll. He tried dragging his fingers through her matted curls; but Kinza objected to this and slapped him. Being very tired and out of sorts he slapped back, at which Kinza set up a loud roar for her mother and her morning bowl of black coffee. She could not understand what was happening or where she was, and in any case she hated being washed. So for a time they sat together by the stream, sniffing and miserable—a weary, haggard-eyed little boy, and an exceedingly cross, tousled baby, looking strangely out of harmony with the fresh world, dew-spangled and bathed in sunrise.

But after a time, having exhausted her rage, Kinza groped toward him with her arms, nestled into his lap, stuck her thumb in her mouth and forgave him. He looked down at her rather desperately. She was so heavy, and his back ached so, but they must get a little farther before the sun grew really hot. So he hauled her up, and set off again, and the path up the mountain seemed to grow steeper and steeper. There was, however, one comfort. The path climbed along the edge of the brook, and every ten minutes or so he stopped to bathe his feet, or walked a little way among the cold cresses that bordered the water. He passed huts nestling in a hollow on his left and little patches of sloping land where ripe corn rustled. He picked a handful of ears to munch on his journey, and climbed on through rocky olive groves, leaving the stream behind him. Kinza, wide awake and enjoying herself, bounced up and down on his back and pum-mulled his aching shoulders, and the sun rose higher, burning his head.

He must stop. If he did not lie down somewhere he felt sure that he would fall asleep as he walked. He looked round, but the whole landscape seemed to swim in front of him. Then beyond the shadows of the olive groves he saw a gleam of gold, and knew he was coming to another little patch of harvest.

He never quite remembered how he arrived, and he never even noticed that the field was dangerously near a village. He crept in among the stems, right into the heart of the corn and lay down with his head resting on his arm, and Kinza curled up in the crook of his knee. Through the rustling canopy of gold above him he caught a glimpse of blue sky; poppies brushed his cheek and lulled him with their drowsy scent. He fell fast, fast asleep, and the field, white already to harvest, gathered him to its bosom, and hid him safely.

Kinza, however, who had slept excellently all night, saw no reason why she should sit in such an uncom-fortable spot all day. At home she wandered where she liked, and cornstalks are prickly. Also, Kinza was very hungry. Her mother had never deserted her before, and was sure to be near at hand if only she could escape from this extraordinary place where things tickled her legs and made her sneeeze. She uncurled herself resolutely and battled ahead, following that sure instinct of hers to travel toward light. She emerged from the corn patch without much difficulty, and stood, listening intently. Then—oh, joy!—her keen ears caught the faint humming of a grindstone not far away. Like the sweet music of his native land to a wanderer was the song of the grindstone to Kinza. Grindstones meant Mother, and Mother meant shelter and food and comfort and security and an end of all strange, rustling, prickly places. With a shrill cry of delight she staggered toward the sound, with outstretched arms.

The woman sitting at the door of her hut heard the cry and looked up. Then she sat staring and staring as though she had seen a ghost, for there lurched toward her on unsteady feet the queerest little figure she had ever seen in her life; it was a tiny child in a dirty cotton gown, her outstretched hands groping, her face lifted to the light. Her curls, matted into a thick black bush, were crowned with a halo of straw. She was covered all over with wheat chaff, and as the woman sat staring at her the apparition began to sneeze.

So as soon as the noise of grinding ceased, Kinza, no longer guided by the sound, and knowing herself

in a strange place, stood irresolute for a moment.
Then she held up her arms, and said one appealing
word—"Ima!" (Mother).

The woman sitting at the grindstone was a young
woman. The previous winter had been a hard one.
Her husband's crop had been poor, and the cow had
sickened; they had been very hungry and very poor.
Her only child had died, and one dark day they had
buried him under the snow. So now, when this baby
staggered toward her and lisped the very word she
had longed to hear for six lonely months, she stopped
neither to reason nor to wonder. She drew the dirty
little creature into her lap, held it tight, and began
crooning over it and kissing it.

Kinza resisted a little at first, and whimpered. She
knew that these were the wrong arms, and that this
woman was not her mother; but after all they were
strong safe arms, and the hand caressing her curls
was a gentle hand. Her stiff little body relaxed, and
she lay at peace and asked for a drink. Her new
friend fetched her a bowl of buttermilk, and Kinza
sat up. Holding the bowl in both hands, she drained
it to the last drop. Then, looking even odder, because
of the white milky rim round her mouth, she curled
up kitten-like in the woman's lap and went to sleep.

It was evening when Hamid woke up and lay wondering where he was. He seemed to be lying in shadow
looking up at a golden roof, where the sloping rays

of light caught the ears of wheat. His body ached, but he felt rested and comfortable. As he lay there it gradually all came back to him; then he sprang up with a little cry of concern.

Where was Kinza?

In spite of his fright he knew he must be cautious, so he crept to the edge of the patch. He could see her tracks, because the wheat was broken and the poppies were crushed. They had come in on the lower side; she had gone out on the upper side, and he peered through the stalks in the direction she must have taken. What he saw was a great surprise.

Not fifty yards from where he crouched stood a hut, and on the step, perfectly at home, and apparently not missing him in the least, sat Kinza, eating cherries. Her foster-mother sat behind her in the doorway, laughing and trying to deal with Kinza's matted curls; and, arranged in a semicircle round them, squatted the whole village. They had turned out to a man to stare at this child, who apparently lived alone, like a rabbit, in the middle of a corn patch, and had accidentally strayed into their midst.

Hamid lay perfectly still, except that the sight of the cherries reminded him how hungry he was, and his hand stole to the loaf. He gnawed it thoughtfully; he was very ashamed of himself. They had lost a whole precious day in sleep and, worst of all, he had let Kinza escape into what might prove to be an enemy camp, unless he could retrieve her very quickly; for these people would certainly come to hear of the missing child from Thursday village. He dared not show himself; they might imprison him for skulking in their corn, and anyhow his only hope of rescue lay in remaining concealed.

So once again the sun went down, and moonlight flooded the village; then, when the world lay perfectly still, there was a tiny rustle in the corn. On silent feet Hamid crossed the open space, and stood poised in the doorway. The woman's husband lay on a mattress, snoring loudly, and his wife slept at his feet. There was no room for Kinza on the mattress, but she had been put to bed on a little mat near the door, and covered with a goat skin.

Hamid stooped down and gathered her up in his arms. She gave a little sigh, and half woke. He breathed her name urgently, and, knowing all was well, she nestled up to him, clinging to him with all her strength. Neither buttermilk nor cherries had had any power to divide her loyalty. Although she had had a pleasant day, she knew something had been vaguely wrong. Now she was safely back in the tired arms of her brother; somehow from the moment he picked her up she slept more soundly than before. She had returned to her right place.

Five minutes later a gasping, frightened little boy with a thumping heart was hurrying up the hillside as fast as he could go, clutching Kinza against him. Not a villager had turned in his sleep, not a dog had

lifted its head or barked. Noiseless as a ghost he had
effected his rescue and Kinza had been perfectly co-
operative.

Then, pausing for an instant to look about him, he
saw a winding strip of stony road on his left, and
made toward it. He looked up to the mountain
towering above him, back to the valley and the river
that led home. Hitching Kinza firmly on to his back,
he set his face steadfastly toward the summit.

CHAPTER SEVEN

A Narrow Escape

HE REACHED the top just before dawn, limping, shivering, and unutterably weary. The nights on that high mountain pass were cold even in summer, and Hamid wore nothing but one coarse cotton gown. Kinza, too, snuggled closer to him, and began coughing and snuffling. He was too tired to go any farther for a while, so he squatted down on the lee side of the

Spanish fort where sentries kept watch on the valley, and waited for morning.

He had left the path before reaching the fort, and had come up quietly at the back, because for all he knew the sentry might keep watch even by night. But all seemed silent and deserted on that lonely outpost, and the two cold children huddled together and longed for the sun to rise.

And once again the daily miracle happened, and the stars grew pale in a violet east. Like two little sunworshipers they sat, longing for its advent. A bird rose up, its wings wet with dew, saw it afar off, and flung back a cry of hope to the waiting earth. Then it came and wrapped the pilgrims round with warmth and healing and comfort. They divided the last of their first loaf, and Hamid rose stiffly to his feet.

The crest was just above him, and the road ran along a high ridge before it started on its downward course. On either side he could look down into deep valleys enclosed by mountains, and beyond the mountains were more mountains—range upon range of rocky peaks flushed by sunrise. Hamid felt as though he were standing alone on top of the world; in a place where no other human foot had ever trod.

There was one spot on the landscape that filled him with concern, and which he determined to avoid at all costs. At the far end of the ridge stood the Tuesday Market, a Spanish settlement with white government buildings, and plenty of idle soldiers on the lookout

for mischief. If by any chance his father had reported
him to the police the night before, they would certainly have 'phoned Tuesday Market to watch the
paths. It was clear that he must leave the path, and
make his way straight down the mountain side
through the scrub bushes and olive groves until he
reached the river in the valley some two thousand
feet below. There he could sleep among the oleanders
until sunset, when it would be safe to take the road
again.

Binding Kinza on to his back again, he stepped
out into the open and almost collided with two men
on horseback, who had ridden up on the other side
of the fort. They were on their way to Tuesday Market, and had traveled by night to escape the heat.

Hamid stood stock still and stared at them stupidly,
too tired to act quickly. They were both from his own
village, and he knew them by sight.

The men stared at him for a moment; they had ridden straight into the sun, and were a little dazzled.
Then one leaped lightly from his horse, and made a
grab at Hamid.

"It's Si Mohamed's boy," he cried, "the one who
was missing from Thursday Market the day before
yesterday."

Hamid ducked and bolted down the mountain side.
His sudden movement startled the horse, which
reared in the air. The man, loath to let go of the reins,
gave an angry shout, and the horse plunged for-

ward. By the time the animal was properly under control the child was far away, leaping through the scrub, with Kinza bumping mercilessly behind him. Unconscious of thorns and roots, forgetful of his cut, bleeding feet, he went careering on, not daring to look behind, always expecting to feel a heavy hand laid on his shoulder and Kinza wrenched away from him.

The merchant, still clinging to the bridle, stood watching him. He had done his best, but he was not going to go chasing somebody else's brat all over the scrub bushes in his bright new yellow shoes with their pointed toes. It was none of his business, and he wanted to be in good time for market. He shrugged his shoulders, mounted his horse and rode on; he would tell the police at Tuesday Market. It was their job, not his, to hunt for runaway boys.

But poor Hamid, hearing in imagination terrible leaping feet behind him, went lumbering on, and Kinza, with her body nearly shaken to bits, gave jerky wails and hiccups on his back. He dared not stop running, and there seemed no refuge. Once he caught his foot in a root and fell headlong. Bruised and dirty, he was up in a second, and as he rose he noticed a rock jutting out ahead of him. He made for it blindly, rounded it, and found himself close to a thatched hut; and beside the hut was a mud goat-shed.

Hamid was quite certain that at any minute his

enemy would appear round the rock, and this was his very last hope of escape. He sprang into the close dark shelter of the goat-shed, and found a sick goat and her kid lying on some straw. There was a pile of provender stacked against the wall, and Hamid burrowed into it. Then, like a hunted rabbit, he lay panting and shivering for half an hour.

At the end of that time, his heart was beating more normally, so he wriggled himself round in the straw, and began to take stock of the situation. From the house in front of the barn he could hear the sound of churning and the shrill prattle of little children, but otherwise all was quiet. His enemy had apparently not pursued him.

He himself felt very ill; he was burning hot, and his head ached dreadfully. His limbs were heavy and stiff, and the straw pricked and chafed his bleeding feet. They had had nothing to drink that morning, and his mouth was parched with fear and running. Kinza too was miserable, and wanted a drink. She had set up a pitiful sort of mewing, like that of a starved kitten, and her brother's pleadings were powerless to silence her. If anyone came to the barn, they would certainly hear her.

He looked round desperately, and then for the first time he began to consider the sick goat, which had broken its front leg some days before, and could not walk to pasture. His spirits went up at once, for here was the solution to their problems. Hamid understood goats, and a mother with a kid would have plenty of milk.

He wormed his way out of the straw, and, stealing to the doorway, grabbed hold of a piece of a broken clay pot that had been thrown away. Then, with one eye on the house, he made friends with the goat, fondling her ears and letting her lick his hands. When she had finally recognized him as the expert that he was, he crept round behind her, and made friends with the kid. Then lying down on the floor beside it he milked the goat into the piece of shard, and carried the milk—sweet, warm, and frothing—to Kinza. She stuck her head out of her straw nest, drank it all up, and mewed for more. Hamid repeated the process a good many times, for the shard did not hold much, and both he and Kinza were parched and starving. They soaked hard pieces of bread in it, and Kinza enjoyed herself immensely, while the kind old goat gave ungrudgingly as though to an extra pair of kids. Once, while they were drinking, a very little girl came in and presented the goat with a bundle of new-mown hay; Hamid held his breath and pulled Kinza down in the straw, and the little girl, her eyes unaccustomed to the gloom, noticed nothing.

The excitement of milking, the pain in his feet, the stuffy heat of the straw pile, and the fever in his own body had kept Hamid wakeful all the morning. He was terrified of going to sleep too, because of Kinza's wandering propensities. He looked round for a piece of rope with which he might tether her to him. There was nothing suitable, and he dared not come out till nightfall. Then sleep suddenly crept over him, dulling his reason and scattering his fears. He clasped her tightly to him, and knew no more.

But his tight grasp relaxed in sleep, and Kinza, taking his deep quiet breathing as a sign that she might now do as she pleased, wriggled out of his arms. She could not understand her brother's sudden liking for these prickly, tickly, hot places that made her sneeze. It was a liking she did not share in the least; and emerging from her hole, spluttering and indignant, she crawled off the provender heap.

Her private exploration yesterday had led her straight to a mother; today she was equally fortunate. She took a few uncertain steps and bumped straight into the goat.

She knew it was a goat instantly by its homely smell and the feel of its rough coat; and if there was one species of creation above all others which Kinza loved and felt perfectly at home with, it was the goat. She groped confidently for its ears and fondled them, after which she cupped her tiny hands round its nose. Then having found what she wanted—friendly company and a place to lie in which did not prick—she crawled under its beard and curled up to sleep, while the little kid, no doubt feeling jealous, also butted its way under its mother's chin. So they lay together, encircled by the goat's front legs: the new-born kid and the lost baby, equally content with their quarters.

Hamid, turning feverishly in his sleep, soon tossed away the straw and lay with his arms and face exposed. The day drew on, and toward sunset the mother of the prattling children came in with a bucket to milk the lame goat. For a moment she thought the creature had had another kid—then she looked more closely, and found it was a little girl curled up in a ball.

"May God have mercy on me!" exclaimed the woman. "It's a baby!"

She looked round in bewilderment, and caught sight of Hamid's top half sticking out of the straw.

"May God have mercy on my parents!" she cried out; "there's a boy as well!"

She strode vigorously over to him and prodded him with her leathery foot. She was a brawny woman, with broad cheek-bones and strong, bowed shoulders. Her voice was loud and strident, and she wanted an explanation quickly.

Hamid woke with a start and struggled into a sitting position. He was fuddled with sleep, but realized at once that where he was he was cornered and caught like a rat in a trap. His head still ached violently, and he lost all control of himself. He stuffed his knuckles into his eyes and began to cry.

"Stop it!" said the woman, slapping him on the back. "You are not from our village. Who are you? and where have you come from?"

Hamid gulped back his sobs, and looked at her. He
had not the smallest objections to telling lies, but in
this case he thought it might be an advantage to tell
the truth. He had noticed that women were usually
ready to take each other's part against husbands, unless, of course, they happened to be the wives of one
man, and this woman would almost certainly side
with his mother. So he told his story just as it stood,
and she listened, frowning and nodding in turn.

When he had finished she looked at him approvingly. It was a good story and seemed true enough.
She had been married twice, and her first husband
had been very cruel to her and her child. He had
divorced her when she was only fifteen years old, so
she was quite ready to take up the cudgels against
husbands in general. She, too, had known what it was
to see her baby ill-treated, and she felt sorry for this
unknown woman who was willing to risk so much for
her blind child.

Besides all this, the woman had a motherly heart,
and this bright-eyed boy who coughed as he spoke
was obviously ill. About the filthy little bundle cud-
dling her goat she knew nothing as yet, but at least
she could give her a better spot to sleep in. So she
milked her goat, and then, with the bucket in her
right hand and Kinza under her left arm, she strode to
her house, with Hamid limping behind her.

The house was a circular mud-hut, rather dark inside, with a stack of winter bedding for the goats

heaped against the wall. A clay pot bubbled on a fire, and three little girls sat round it expectantly. As they entered, the husband came down the mountain side with the flock, and they all gathered round to eat. Hamid, who had eaten nothing but bread and milk for two days, thought he had never tasted anything so good—a lentil stew, flavored with garlic, oil, and red pepper—hunks of hot, soft bread to dip in it—a bowl of buttermilk from which they all drank in turn —and finally a dish of bruised apricots—the unbruised ones the father would carry to the Wednesday Market at dawn next day.

Hamid, eating and drinking deeply, felt his strength come back to him; for one night at least he would be safe and sheltered, and the peace of that knowledge cured his headache. The brawny countrywoman sat licking her fingers, and he gazed up at her as though she were a kind of angel from Heaven.

After supper the three little girls curled themselves up on goatskins against the hay, and went straight to sleep, in company with a cat and three kittens which also slept on a goatskin up against the hay. The father went out to milk, and his wife followed because she wanted to talk to him. Hamid, sitting by the fire with Kinza leaning up against him, could hear their voices. He supposed they were talking about him, and he was quite right, for the woman came back soon after with everything fixed up.

"Don't be afraid," she said encouragingly; "my hus-

band is quite willing to help you. He is going into
Wednesday Market tomorrow to sell apricots. He
picks up a market truck at the bottom of the hill just
before daybreak. He will take you with him, and say
you are my sister's children, for my sister lives on the
road to Friday Market, where you are trying to get
to, and she has a boy about your age and a baby girl.
The truck will drop you about one and a half miles
from Friday Market, on the main road, and you can
probably get a lift—if not, it's not too far to walk."

She looked down at his joyful face, flushed in the
firelight, and suddenly felt sorry because he was so
young and helpless. Like Another long ago, she
fetched a basin of water and a towel, and stooping
down she washed his bruised, cut feet. Then she tore
up a rag into strips, and bound up his wounds with
olive oil; finally she laid him on one sheepskin with
his little sister, and covered him warmly with another.
He fell asleep instantly, grateful and unafraid, and she
went and sat very still on her doorstep, her hands
folded, looking out into the dusk. A strange hush
seemed to have fallen over her; she felt as though
some sweet, unknown Presence had entered her
dwelling, brooding over her and the sleeping children.

Who knows? It is written in the Bible, "Whosoever
shall receive one such little child in my name receiv-
eth Me."

"And His Name is Love."

CHAPTER EIGHT

Hamid's Success

TWENTY-FOUR HOURS later Hamid stood gazing up at the walls of the city he had come so far to seek, and feeling more lost than he had ever felt in his life before.

The journey had been lonely in parts, but after all Hamid was a shepherd, used to mountain solitudes. Wide skies and unpeopled distances held no terrors for him, and he was quite used to his own company. But this mass of humanity and mules and goats jostling each other in the town gate, and the crowd of ragged children all perfectly at home, appalled him. His was the loneliness of the stranger—in the city, but not of it.

He had had a very successful day. He had awakened at cock-crow, cool and refreshed; the woman had fed them and blessed them, and sent them forth into the dawn with her husband. At the bottom of the hill a truck, jammed tight with marketgoers and their wares, had picked them up and rattled off down the valley. Hamid had never been in a truck before and the noise and speed and jolting thrilled him. He squatted in a corner, holding Kinza, trying to look like his benefactor's sister-in-law's son, and watching the river and the mountain landscape. The main road thrilled him too, with its roaring vehicles, and the two hours' drive passed all too quickly. The road turned off to Wednesday Market, and he and Kinza were dropped about fifteen miles from their destination.

He had walked all day, patiently plodding along in the heat, often sitting down to rest. At one point the river flowed parallel to the road, and here an idea had occurred to him. He had sat Kinza to sunbathe behind a bush, and washed her little dress as best he could, spreading it out to dry in the sun; for it struck him, when he looked at her critically, that nobody was going to be really pleased to see Kinza any more, unless she could be made a little cleaner. The result was encouraging, and Hamid redressed her, patted her tangles, washed her face, and decided she looked fit for a palace.

He had then climbed a long, long hill, with cornfields sweeping away to the valley and bright flowers nodding on the banks. He picked a bunch of poppies and other flowers for Kinza to present to her new mother, and toiled on gazing up at the mountain on his right. He did not like it. His own mountains were clothed with grass and rounded, with gentle slopes, but these were stark and bare, with summits of jagged rock. Yet the meadows at their skirts were greener than any meadows he had seen before, and the harvests more golden. He wondered why, and then forgot to wonder, for he had rounded a bend in the road and just ahead of him was the old city wall and the town inside—tier upon tier of lichened tiled roofs clustering round white mosques, rising steeply to the rock behind them. Down below were the white buildings of the Spanish settlement built round a square.

Hamid stood in the cool shadow of the gate, and watched for a while. He did not think he would have to ask the way if he could once find the market, for his mother had described the house exactly, and he felt afraid to speak to anyone. He thought he would wait until nightfall before venturing along those narrow, crowded, cobbled streets. It would be easier to slip along in the dark. But as dusk deepened he saw

the shopkeepers on each side of the street turn on the
lights, and all who passed by walked in the full glare
of them. Apparently in this terrifying place there was
no darkness and no hiding. The sooner he could safely
get rid of Kinza the better.

He set off timidly along the cobbles, marveling at
the beautiful wares displayed in the shops—the bright
silks and high-colored sweetmeats, the piles of
fruit and stacks of bread. It seemed to him like fairy-
land. He gazed, bright-eyed and fascinated, at all this
beauty—a magic town where everything glittered and
dazzled, where perhaps no one was ever ill or sad or
hungry or cold. He forgot he had felt lonely and
afraid, and gazed up eagerly into the faces of the
shopkeepers and passers-by, bathed in the warmth
and light. But no one smiled at him or looked kindly
at him, and no one welcomed him to the golden city.

He crept along until he came to a splashing fountain where a little girl was filling buckets. She at least
looked like a kind little girl and very shyly he asked
the way to the inn above the market. She pointed
down some cobbled steps, gave him directions, and
disappeared through her own front door.

It was not far to the inn. The old archway leading
into the courtyard stood back from the street, but
weary mules and donkeys were passing in, and travelers stood in groups looking out on the market.
Hamid longed to go and rest in the straw, because he
would have felt at home with the donkeys, but he had

no coin to pay for such shelter; and besides, he felt his busines had better be done that night.

He was to go up the street directly opposite the inn. It was a very short street, ending in a wall; and the house, so his mother had said, was the very last on the left, with only a rubbish heap beyond it. It could not be difficult to find, and he set off confidently.

Then the street curved and he stopped. He could see to the end now, and what he saw filled him with surprise.

There was a dim street lamp outside the last house on the left, and under it he could see a group of little boys, dirty and ragged like himself, standing expectantly. As Hamid watched, the house was opened from within, and a beam of bright light shone out on to the cobbles. At the turning of the key the children surged forward, tumbling over each other, and disappeared through the golden doorway. Then he heard other footsteps behind him. Three more little boys in black tatters sped past him on swift, bare feet; they too entered in. Then, as Hamid still stood in the shadows staring at the broad beam of light in the street, he heard the sound of singing—shrill unmusical singing it would have sounded to most readers of this story, but Hamid thought he had never heard anything so beautiful.

Lured by the music he crept closer, skulking along the wall. At last he reached the step and dared to peep in. Then he caught his breath with joy and ex-

citement, for he was looking across a passage-way
into another room, and hanging on the wall of that
room exactly opposite the doorway was the picture
of the Man who loved little children, carrying in His
arms a baby just about Kinza's age. Boys and girls
were flocking round Him, holding out their arms, and
He smiled down on them and did not seem to want
them to go away. Hamid remembered the hard faces
of the shopkeepers; this Man was unlike any of them.
He would certainly welcome Kinza just as He was
welcoming the crowd of happy children in the picture.

But who were all those ragged little boys? and why
did they go in? and what were they singing about?
He could not see them, for they all gathered at one
end of the room, but he could hear a woman's voice
speaking; and as he listened, crouching on the step,
straining to catch the words, the children within began to chant something all together, as though they
were learning it by heart, just as they did in the
mosque schools when they learned the Koran.

Yes, he could hear what they were saying now—
wonderful glowing words, brighter than any ever
written in the Koran:

"Jesus said, I am the light of the world: he that followeth me shall not walk in darkness, but shall have
the light of life."

What could it mean? Three times through they repeated the verse, and Hamid whispered the words

with them, and tucked them away in his memory to think about afterward. The immediate problem now was, what to do about Kinza?

If all these children belonged to the nurse, she would certainly not want another; no little girls had entered the house, so perhaps the English, like his own people, preferred boys. Kinza's chances seemed very small if he knocked at the door and presented her as a gift. He must think of a better way than that.

Then a plan presented itself to him which he thought would almost certainly be successful, because his mother had said that the Saint in the picture had never been known to turn a child away. He would simply leave Kinza in the passage like a surprise parcel to explain herself as best she might and, if this nurse was really like her Saint, she too could be depended upon; she would not throw such a tiny helpless creature homeless into the street on a dark night.

He skipped across the orange beam and established himself on the rubbish heap; he shook Kinza until she was thoroughly wide awake and then spoke to her very solemnly.

"Kinza, little sister," he said, "I am going to sit you down by yourself, and you must keep very still, and not cry. If you cry a lady will beat you hard. If you don't cry she will soon come and give you a nice sweet."

Now this was language that Kinza understood perfectly. She knew all about being hit if she did not keep still, and she seldom got what she wanted by crying. Also she was very hungry. So she submitted herself to being smoothed and patted and uncrumpled as much as possible, and then Hamid placed the withered bunch of flowers in her hand and crept off the rubbish heap. He pushed the door open another inch, lifted Kinza over the step, and sat her down in the dark passage.

All was perfectly quiet inside except for the voice within. Hamid suddenly felt his throat tighten and his eyes filled. Kinza would never be his own again, and he realized how much he loved her. As a sign of his love he drew out his last dry crust from the cloth, and thrust it into her hand; then he left her sitting cross-legged against the wall, very tousled and very crumpled, clasping a bunch of dead poppies and an old crust, for the surprise and delight of the unsuspecting missionary.

But through the blur of his tears he had caught sight once again of the face of the Man in the picture. He seemed to be looking straight at Kinza. Hamid felt he had left his little sister sitting in the light of that smile, and it comforted him. Of course, the beams came through the open doorway of the lighted room, and it was only in his imagination that they streamed from that Person. Then, crouching against the wall of a little alley leading off the street, he tried to remember the words he had heard three times over: "Jesus said, I am the light of the world . . . instead of darkness you can have the light of life." It was something like that, and what ever could it mean?

What was the light of the world? He thought of the lamp burning in his hut at home and the flickering shadows on the wall. He remembered the moonlit journey, and the circling stars, and the sunrise on top of the mountain. Moonlight, starlight, sunlight, candlelight, and the orange glare of the city streets—they had all faded now. He was sitting alone in a very dark alley, and the moon had not yet risen behind the wall of rock. But Jesus said that instead of darkness you can have the light of life. "I am the light of the world." He thought of Kinza and her perpetual darkness—could this light which he had never seen ever reach her? what did it all mean? If only it wasn't so dark . . . if only he wasn't so hungry . . . if only he could have kept Kinza . . . if only he could run home to his mother.

He stopped short in his thoughts, and leaned forward eagerly. A crowd of boys came hurrying down the street, and, at the corner, silhouetted against the window of a house, they turned to wave. They were talking eagerly, all at once, so Hamid could not hear what they said, but he caught odd phrases: "Who is she?"—"Such a little girl"—"Where is her mother?" Then they passed out of sight, and the street was left in silence.

Then, prompted by his great longing to see what had happened, he tiptoed out of his alley, and prowled back to the rubbish heap. The door to which he had taken her was fast shut, and all was silence within. What had happened? There was a light in an upper window, and Hamid crossed the street and stood with his back pressed against the wall of the house opposite, gazing upward. As he stood looking there passed across the lighted window the figure of a woman nestling a little child in her arms, and the child showed no signs of fear. It neither struggled nor cried. It lay at peace with one little hand uplifted to feel the face bowed over it.

He had accomplished his errand and fulfilled his vow. All was well with Kinza. Not knowing where else to go, he slunk back to the rubbish heap, and, covering himself as best he could with his rags, he curled up against the wall to sleep, with his head pillowed on his arm. In his dreams he thought he saw Kinza being carried safely through the dark in the light of one clear ray; and whether they were the arms of the woman that held her so safe or the arms of the One in the picture he never could tell. Only he knew for certain, without any doubt at all, that the light would never grow dim, and the arms would never, never let her go.

CHAPTER NINE

Hamid's New Friends

HAMID AWOKE early next morning, stiff and cold, and blamed himself for his rashness in sleeping so near the house. Yet somehow it comforted him to know that Kinza was so close to him, only separated perhaps by one thickness of brick and plaster. He wondered whether she had awakened yet, and what she was doing. He wandered along the street and out into the deserted market, wondering what to do, where to go, and above all where his breakfast was coming from. He had no doubt that Kinza was feeding on the fat of the land and rather regretted having given her that last crust.

It looked a golden city no longer. The shops were shuttered, and a few homeless beggars lay up against the temple steps, still fast asleep. Now that he had done all he had come to do, Hamid felt horribly flat and tired, and he stood in the middle of the market longing for home.

Then into the midst of his longing broke a familiar sound—the harsh rattle of a stork's cry and the rush of great wings sweeping over him, just as they used to do when he led his herd to pasture on his own dear mountains. He looked up quickly and saw her high up with the morning shining on her wings, flying to her nest in the grey turret of an old fort. He watched her alight, and saw the upthrust of the baby beaks gobbling their food. The sight of them eased his loneliness a little, for the storks were part of home —only in his village they nested in the thatches and here their home was in a castle. He had not noticed this castle before, and now he looked at it with interest. He did not know that it was about five hundred years old, but he thought it looked very ancient and crumbling, and wondered whether anyone else lived in it besides the storks. He stared at the massive old walls and found that he was standing opposite an old gate in an archway leading into a garden.

The gate was wide open and there seemed no one to stop him. Hamid trotted across the cobbles, climbed the steps, and tiptoed through; he found himself standing in the most beautiful place he had ever seen in his life. It was a square garden enclosed in four grey walls over which the wistaria hung in great curtains. In the middle of it was a fountain, surrounded by green lawns and flowerbeds, which were a scented mass of color. Snapdragons, pansies, and stocks all grew in a riot, and behind them were rose bushes and orange trees in blossom. The roses were of every color—crimson, apricot, and pale pink in every stage of unfolding—and the air was heavy with fragrance. Never before had Hamid even dreamed of such beauty, and he stood fascinated with clasped hands, trying to take it all in. Then, as no one appeared to chase him, he wandered along the little paths breathing in the scent of orange blossom, until he came to a cage set in the wall, where behind the bars stood a lordly male peacock, its tail spread wide, and its little brown wives standing reverently round.

If the garden was the most beautiful thing Hamid had ever seen, the peacock's tail was certainly the most wonderful; he stood for a full twenty minutes simply staring. Then he walked on, and as he walked something happened. The sun rose behind the wall of rock, and in an instant the whole garden was transfigured. The dew on the roses turned to glittering silver and the petals of the orange blossom looked sud-

denly transparent. Hamid, dazzled, rubbed his fingers
in his eyes, and there flashed into his mind for the
first time that morning the half-forgotten words of
the night before: "Jesus said, I am the light of the.
world . . . no more darkness . . . the light of life."
Then he looked up again at the transformed garden
and laughed aloud. The upturned faces of the pansies
seemed to laugh with him, and a rainbow shimmered
about the fountain. But in the midst of his ectasy a
keeper entered through the archway, and ordered
him out. He really had no right to do so, for they were
public gardens, but Hamid had yet to learn that in
the city all ragged little boys, even quite harmless
ones, were looked upon with suspicion.

He went away rather sadly through an archway
in another wall, and found himself in an open cobbled
space bounded by a building that looked to him like
a king's palace, but was, in reality, a hotel. The town
was beginning to wake up now, and men were un-
shuttering their stalls. Herdsmen were selling their
milk, and as Hamid stood watching there was wafted
to his nose a delicious smell of fried batter and hot
oil. He was so hungry that something inside him
seemed to turn right over, and he looked round
eagerly to discover where it came from.

He had been standing with his back to a little stall
where a man was frying dough-rings in a deep stone
trough of oil. He seemed a busy man, for, as well as

having to fish out the crinkly dough rings and string them on to blades of grass for his customers, he was having to blow up the fire underneath—which appeared to put him in a bad temper, for he was muttering and growling a good deal.

Hamid drew as near as he dared to that delicious smell and stood first on one foot and then on the other. Then he suddenly had an idea: he walked boldly forward, feeling almost desperate with hunger, and asked the man if he needed an assistant.

The man looked him up and down. The boy who usually helped him had not turned up that morning, and it was making life very difficult for Sillam, the doughnut-maker. He was prepared to accept help from the first boy who turned up, and Sillam had never seen this one before. He could not say that he actually knew him to be a rogue and a thief. He opened the wooden barrier and motioned Hamid inside.

"Take the bellows," he said, "and blow up this fire, and if I find you helping yourself to anything that doesn't belong to you, the police station is opposite!"

Hamid squatted down and began to blow. He did not feel very well; it was so hot that the air swam and quivered round him, and the leaping flames scorched his face. He did not know that many little boys before him had been unable to stand the heat, and that he was pleasing the master by his quiet endurance. The fire roared upward, the oil hissed and crackled in the cauldron. Then from what seemed a long way away he heard the master's voice saying, "Enough," and he staggered to his feet, dizzy and flushed.

"Now stand here, and thread the dough rings on to the reeds," said the master, and Hamid leaned gratefully forward, taking deep breaths of air. He worked deftly enough, burning his fingers a little, but not minding much because he was too hungry to think about anything but the gnawing pains inside him. But he did notice that the market place was filling up, and that quite a crowd of tattered, grimy little boys were lounging about, watching him with searching eyes. He realized that somehow, before long, he would have to give an account of himself.

He had worked for about two hours, when the master suddenly said, "Have you had any breakfast?"

"No," said Hamid, "and, last night, no supper."

The master handed him a couple of hot, golden dough-rings. With a great sigh of relief Hamid sank his teeth into the first. It was wonderful. But the dark eyes of the little boys sitting on the cobbles became suddenly hostile. They were hungry, too, and this stranger was holding a coveted position.

Dough-rings are a breakfast food, and the shop shut at mid morning. The master told Hamid he had worked well and might return early next day. Then he gave him a small coin, and Hamid, feeling like a little king, strutted across the market to decide how he would spend his wealth. He noticed a pile of sticky green sweets, and longed to buy one for Kinza. But Kinza probably no longer needed green sweets, and, in the comfort of her new home, had perhaps forgotten all about him. His throat suddenly felt a little tight. He resolutely stopped thinking about her, and turned his attention to the baker's shop.

It was then that a voice at his side said, "Who are you?" and he turned to see a little boy about his own age with a shaved, spotted head and a garment that had once been white, made from a printed sugar-sack. A strange little figure—but his dark eyes were bright and intelligent, and he looked at Hamid in quite a friendly way.

Hamid faced the little boy shyly. "I'm from the country," he replied.

"Why have you come to town?"

"To find work."

"Where are your father and mother?"

"Dead."

"Where do you live?"

"In the street."

The little citizen, whose name was Ayashi, nodded approvingly. "I too," he said cheerfully, "have no mother, and my father has gone to the mountains. I too live in the streets, and so do some of those other boys sitting under the tree. Now buy us a loaf with the money the master gave you, and give us each a piece. Then you shall be one of us, and we will show you where we go for a supper at night."

His confident tone and his cheery acceptance of his homelessness fascinated Hamid. He would have flung his coin at the boy's feet in order to secure such a friendship. "You shall be one of us" were wonderful words; Hamid bought his loaf quickly and spent the change on a handful of black, bitter olives. Then he followed his patron to the eucalyptus tree in the middle of the square, where the gang squatted in the shade. He handed over the food to be divided up, and they fell upon it eagerly. Hamid, with his portion, sat a little apart through shyness; but although no one said "Thank you," the willing gift had done its work. From that day onward he was truly one of them.

It was a strange gang to which, in his heart, he swore allegiance that day—a gang bound together by a common bond of dirt, ignorance, and poverty; their uniform—rags and tatters; children who had never been loved; waifs who had never been sheltered. Tough and hardy they were, through much exposure; crafty and quick, through living by their wits. Thieving, lying, and swearing were regular habits, yet they were still merry and courageous at heart, undaunted by hunger and bitter winters, bravely making the most of their meager pleasures. This unexpected meal was enough to make them radiantly happy, and they sat munching and chuckling with their toes tucked under them like a crowd of monkeys. Hard yesterdays were all forgotten, and there was no need to think about tomorrow just yet. Today was a good day, and they were enjoying themselves.

Hamid, watching silently, swelled with pride, because he was sitting among them. Reared with simple country children, he had never met boys like these, and he thought them wonderful--so unashamedly dirty, so tough and devil-may-care, so manly and independent. He longed to become like them, and he wriggled nearer in order to study their conversation and learn their ways.

He gathered that they earned their living by various means. Some worked at looms certain days a week; and others, like himself, helped in the dough-ring shops. All begged between whiles, and hung round the hotel on the chance of carrying a bag for a tourist or watching a car. Some slept with their families at night in hovels called home, while others crept into the mosques. Life was uncertain and exciting, and there seemed only one event in their day which could really be depended on. That was their supper at the house of the English nurse.

Now they were all discussing the extraordinary things that had happened there on the previous night. It was a little stranger girl, they said, and none of them had ever seen her before. No one knew where she came from; she held up her arms to the English nurse and called for her mother, but she would not say anything else. So the English nurse had picked her up and taken her in, and today she was going to seek for the baby's parents.

"And what if she doesn't find them?" asked one little boy. "Will she put her out in the street?"

Ayashi looked up quickly.

"She will not," he replied with complete confidence.

"How do you know? why not? It is not her child!" exclaimed the other children in chorus.

"Because," answered Ayashi simply, "she has a clean heart."

CHAPTER TEN

Supper at the Nurse's House

THE REST OF THE DAY passed pleasantly. Ayashi, pleased by Hamid's admiration, took him round the town and up on to the hillside by the top gate to show him the spring of water welling up from the heart of the mountain through the cleft of a great rock. When all other streams fail through drought, this water, hidden so deep, goes on springing up in

an ice-cold torrent, so that there are splashing fountains in the streets of the town, and a well-watered
countryside. Hamid understood now why the fields
had looked so green and the harvests so golden on the
evening when he first entered the city.

At midday they hung round the door of the hotel;
after a time a waiter flung them some broken rolls
and meat that guests had left on their plates, and the
boys fell upon them like hungry dogs. Then they
curled themselves against the trunk of the eucalyptus
tree and slept in the shade.

Evening came, the sun set behind the turret of the
fort, and the mother stork stood on one leg, clear-cut
against a rosy sky. Hamid stuck close to Ayashi, and
they sat on some steps together with a few friends
watching the country people crowding into the
square. Tomorrow was market day, and those who
had come from a distance would spread out their
sacks against the wall and sleep beside their wares.
As darkness fell the shopkeepers kindled their lamps
again, and other little boys sauntered up from their
various employments and collected on the steps.

"Come," said Ayashi, who seemed to be a sort of
leader among them, "she will soon open her door
now."

He motioned Hamid to follow him, but Hamid
hesitated. He felt torn in two; hunger and his great
longing to see whether all was well with his little sister
urged him on, but caution held him back. What if he

should be forced to speak in Kinza's presence? She
would certainly recognize his voice and run to him,
and that would arouse everyone's suspicion.

"Come on," called Ayashi impatiently, looking
back.

Hamid shook his head. "I'm not coming," he replied
and sat down again on the steps, with his head in his
hands, staring gloomily into the market. He had been
fairly happy all day long in Ayashi's company, but
now he forgot Ayashi in his overwhelming longing
for his mother and Kinza. He blamed himself bitterly
for his stupidity in refusing to go with the children.
He might at least have caught sight of her, and he
would have known whether she was happy or not; he
would have heard her prattling voice, and he wanted
to hear it so badly . . . it was worth any risk to see
her again.

He got up, because he had suddenly had an idea.
He would not go in, but he would creep to the door
of the house, as he had done on the night before, and
peep through a crack. Perhaps he would catch a
glimpse of Kinza, or see her again against the orange
window upstairs. Like some guilty little thief he
darted into the quiet back street and sneaked along
the wall toward the open door and the beam of light.

He peered round very cautiously, but there was no
sign or sound of her—only the murmuring voices, and
then the shrill cracked noise of little boys singing.
Kinza apparently was nowhere about, and he was

standing in a very dangerous position. He shuffled on to the rubbish heap, and began to cry quietly because his friends and his little sister had all entered in through the open door that led to shelter and light and food—and he was left outside.

And then something happened. The door opened a little farther, and the nurse stepped out into the street to see if any more were coming along before she started the lesson. She appeared silently, and Hamid did not see her at first. But she heard a wretched, sniffing sound close at hand and looked round.

She saw a desolate little outcast huddled on the rubbish heap with its kunckles in its eyes, and she took a step nearer. He heard her footfall and started up frightened. But she stood between him and freedom and he could not escape, so he rubbed away his tears and crouched staring up at her. He had never seen anyone like her before.

"Why don't you come in?" she asked.

Lured by a sense of welcome, he got up and advanced slowly toward her. She waited quite still, afraid of startling him. Then, when he was close to her, she held out her hand. He took it in his grimy little paw, and stepped trustfully over the threshold.

They entered the lighted room together, and Hamid stood in the doorway taking a good look round. It was a long whitewashed room, furnished Moorish fashion with a rush mat on the floor and mattresses

against the walls. At one end were a table and some
shelves with rows of bottles on them, and at the other
end the boys sat cross-legged in a semicircle. On the
wall opposite the door was the picture of the One
smiling down on these waifs of the street, just as He
had smiled down on Kinza.

"Come," said the nurse, "sit down with the others.
I'm going to show you something."

Ayashi grinned at him delightedly, and Hamid
wormed his way into the semicircle so as to sit beside
him. He wished they would sing again, because he
wanted to hear what they were singing about, but apparently the singing was over, and they were all waiting for the nurse to show them something. Hamid
glanced at their expectant faces and felt less in awe
of them than he had felt all day. They looked somehow younger and more frail. They had seemed like
men of the world before, but now, just for half an
hour or so, they were merely needy children, robbed
of their childhood, listening to a sweet, sweet story
which told of a love and a shelter and a security that
they had never known.

The nurse sat down on the mattress in front of
them, and showed them a strange little book. It was
quite unlike the Koran, which was the only book
Hamid had ever seen inside, and it had no writing in
it at all—which was just as well, because not one of
the audience could read a letter. It had only four
blank pages in it and each page was a different color.

The first page was shining gold and very beautiful, and as the nurse held it up in front of them she spoke of a golden city bright with the light of the love of God, and Hamid thought of his first night in the town when the lamps had shone out in the dark. But in spite of the lamps there were hunger and sickness and loneliness and unkindness in their town, while in the City of God, so the nurse said, there were none of these things—only pure joy and brightness and goodness.

"I'd like to go there," thought Hamid; "it would be even better than our village—no fear, no quarreling, no blindness."

But while he was thinking about the Golden City the nurse turned to a black page and told them it was like the darkness and the sadness of hearts that had done wrong. Hamid had never worried about doing wrong before—in fact, had never even thought what wrong was. Of course, he stole if he got the chance, and naturally he told lies if they would save him a beating—why shouldn't he? Well, one reason seemed to be that no darkness could ever enter the Golden City of light, and the gate was shut to sin.

Hamid looked thoughtfully around the semicircle— how very black they all were! Their rags and their hands and faces and feet were black with dust and grease and mud. Their hearts, said the nurse, were also black with lies and bad words and blows and stealing. That was a pity, thought Hamid, and he had a vision of a host of dirty little boys being turned away from the gates, and creeping back into the shadows.

But that was not the end. The nurse turned to a red page, and told them a very strange story. Apparently God's Son, whose name was Jesus, loved black little boys, and actually wanted them in His bright city. So He had come down into the world to live with them, and then at the end He had died to bear punishment for sins He had never done Himself. It was the children who had sinned, and Jesus who had been punished. The red page meant that He had died a cruel death, and the red blood had flowed from His body—and it did not seem right at all, because *He* had not done anything wrong. It was the children who really deserved the punishment.

The best of this story was that, because Jesus had been punished, bad, black, thieving children could be forgiven. If they turned from sin and asked to be forgiven because Jesus had taken their punishment, their black hearts would be made just like the next page— and the next page was spotless white; they would be made white enough to walk right into the light of the Golden City, and even that radiance would discover no spot. They could be made perfectly pure and clean. Hamid forgot about himself and his black little friends—he thought of the orange blossom petals transparent with the brightness of the sun, and the wings of the stork when the light touched them. Then he forgot all about everything, for the nurse had stopped talking and was bringing in two great bowls of steaming rice and handing round hunks of bread. The children broke into two groups and huddled over their supper, scooping up the food at an amazing pace, and then polishing the bowls with their dirty little fingers. No one spoke much until the last lick and crumb had vanished because they were racing each other to get the most, but when all had gone they sat back on their heels and questioned the nurse about the little girl whom they had found in the hall the night before.

"She is still with me," said the nurse, smiling a little, as though she had remembered something funny. "She is, at this moment, asleep in bed."

Hamid looked at her hard. She did not seem annoyed at Kinza's being still with her.

"I have taken her all round the town with me to-day," went on the nurse, "but nobody has ever seen her before, or knows who her parents are. She is a little blind girl, so I suppose no one wants her."

"And what will you do with her?" asked the boys, all together.

"Well, I shall have to keep her for a time; there's nothing else to be done," said the nurse. This time she laughed outright, and Hamid nearly laughed too, with joy and relief. He had a wild, reckless longing to see his little sister asleep in bed, and he was no longer afraid. He waited until the little boys had

bowed and shaken hands with their hostess and
skipped off into the dark. Then she turned and found
him lingering in the hall. His heart was beating violently, but he spoke steadily and boldly.

"I come from a village," he said, "and in my village
there are two or three blind baby girls whose parents
come into market. Let me see her, and perhaps I can
tell you who her mother is."

The nurse looked down at him, surprised; he might
be speaking the truth. She had watched him since he
entered her house, and noticed his thin, tired face,
and his bruised feet—also the ravenous way he had
eaten his food. She guessed he had traveled a long
way, and was glad to shelter him, so she led him to a
room upstairs, to where Kinza lay on a mattress fast
asleep.

She looked different because she had had a bath
and had come out quite another color. Also her hair
had been washed and cut, and instead of tangles she
had soft dark curls clustering over her forehead. Her
old dress had been changed for a little white night-
gown, spotlessly clean. Surely, thought Hamid, she is
clean enough even to stand in the light of the Heav-
enly City, clean as a white flower; he gazed at her,
fascinated for a while, and then turned to take notice
of her surroundings. The room was furnished simply,
native style, but there were pretty covers on the mattresses, books on the shelves and pictures on the walls.
It was a brightly lit room, too, and he felt as if Kinza

had somehow passed beyond him, through golden gates into a new land of light. He yearned to stay with her, but he knew it could not be. He glanced down at his rags, and knew himself as a black little outcast, with no part in this beautiful place.

"I do not know her," he said gravely, rising to go. "She is not one of the children from our village."

He followed the nurse downstairs in silence, and she came to the door and let him out. He stepped into the street, and then, standing on the boundary of light and darkness, he looked up into her face and took hold of the hand that had been so kind to Kinza.

"You are good!" he said simply. "Your food is good; your teaching is good; your heart is good; may God have mercy upon your ancestors!"

Then he bounded away down the street, and the darkness swallowed him up.

CHAPTER ELEVEN

Two Broken Eggs

H AMID KEPT HIS POST in the doughnut shop and became a satisfactory little assistant. He worked hard, and his master was usually quite kind to him, giving him his breakfast and his coin regularly. The coin he spent on dinner, and the nurse provided him with his supper. He slept with Ayashi just inside the mosque, and as long as the sun shone and the weather kept warm he was happy. Life was gay and varied

and there was plenty to do. During the harvest they
went down to the fields and helped carry the bundles
to the threshing floor till darkness fell, and then they
went to sleep on a heap of chaff. Later on they hired
themselves out to pick olives, stuffing as many as they
could into their mouths without being seen. On hot
days they went bathing in the rocky stream that
flowed from the spring in the mountain, and washed
all their dirt away. When they went to supper with
the nurse those nights she did not at first recognize
them.

Five days a week they went to the house of the
English nurse, and squatted on the mat to hear a
story about Jesus, and to have supper. Hamid knew
quite a number of stories now. He knew that Jesus
was not a Saint at all, but the Son of God, and had
come down into the world. He knew that the lame
and the halt and the blind had flocked to Jesus, and
He had healed them. Hamid wished that he also had
lived then, for he would have carried Kinza to the
Saviour, and her eyes would have been opened. He
knew that Jesus had died with His arms stretched out
in welcome on a cross, and like their saints He had
been placed in a rocky tomb—but with this difference:
their own saints remained in their tombs to be visited
every year, but Jesus had not been bound by death.
He had come to life again and left His tomb, and
had been seen in a beautiful garden, like the castle
garden at sunrise, on the first day of the week.

He knew too that Jesus had gone back to the Golden City and was still alive at the right hand of God, and that the living Spirit of Jesus was willing to enter into the hearts of little boys. Once the nurse spoke about Him knocking at the door of their hearts, and Hamid laid his small dirty hand across his chest under his rags.

"I can hear Him," he said very seriously: "He is knocking at mine . . . tap! tap! tap!"

But the nurse explained that that was his own heart beating, and that the knocking of the Lord could not be felt with hands, nor heard by ear. It was the longing that came over us to open the door that made us know He was knocking; but Hamid by this time was wondering what they were going to have for supper, and he had lost interest in the subject for the time being.

Summer drew into autumn, and the nights became colder and longer. In the valley east of the town the silver birches turned golden and began to shed their leaves; then came the first rainfall, and the farmers blessed God as they thought of their cracked furrows and parched fields; but the beggars in the town hated it. They drew their damp rags around them, and crouched under the archways in the wall, shivering and growling.

There were no more tourists at the hotel now, so there were no cars to watch and no luggage to hold;

these had given quite a lot of money to Hamid and his friends during the summer, but now they must sharpen their wits and tighten their belts. Ayashi taught Hamid the queer, unchildlike beggars' cries, and they would tramp round together in the rain, wailing at the studded wooden doors of rich people's houses. Sometimes they collected a good many scraps of food, sometimes nothing. It was all very uncertain, like the November weather and the temper of the dough-ring man. The only comfort in life that could really be depended on was supper at the house of the English nurse.

She lit a charcoal brazier for them these nights, and let them in early. They would troop across her hall, their rags dripping, leaving a trail of black water and footprints on the tiles. Then they would huddle round the glowing coals to warm their blue fingers, and gradually their teeth would stop chattering. Then they would sit back, steaming a little, but content— and ready to listen to anything their friend might wish to say.

Clothes were a great problem just now. The wind and rain pierced and rotted their rags, and Hamid sometimes wondered just how much longer his flimsy summer garment would hold together, as he saw no prospect of replacing it when it finally fell to pieces. Some of his friends had begged or stolen sacks which they wrapped round them, but Hamid had not been one of the fortunate ones.

Kinza, on the other hand, had no clothes problem. She always went shopping with the English nurse, and Hamid often saw her waddling across the market on legs that had grown amazingly fat and sturdy during the past two months. Over her clean Moorish gown she wore a red woolly jersey and a little brown cloak. She had rubber shoes on her feet and a woolly hood over her dark curls. She looked the picture of health and happiness, and Hamid, edging up as close as possible, felt immensely proud of her.

The rain was coming down mercilessly one night when the children splashed their way up the running cobbles and hammered at the door of their refuge. They shook themselves on the step like wet little dogs, and surged forward toward the fire, puffing and blowing and sniffing. The English nurse felt a pang as she watched them, for she thought she had never seen them looking more wretched, more mud-bespattered, more at enmity with life. Yet the faces lifted to hers were still merry and impudent, and the dark eyes were still bright; she marveled at their unconquered courage.

But there was one well-known little figure missing, and this was the second night he had not turned up —an undersized shrimp of a boy who had been most regular for months past. "Where is Abd-el-Khader?" asked the nurse. "Why hasn't he come these two nights?"

"He can't come," replied one child in a careless voice. "His rags fell right to pieces, and he hasn't a father. He has nothing to wear at all, and he must stay at home till his mother can save enough to buy a sugar-sack."

No one showed any concern or surprise, and the evening passed as usual. But in front of the nurse's eyes there floated the vision of a cold little boy shivering in a dark hut, clasping a bundle of worn-out tatters, and when supper was finished she turned to Hamid, who always lingered to the last. "Do you know where Abd-el-Khader lives?" she asked.

Hamid nodded. "Up at the top of the town by the prickly pear hedges," he replied; "but the path is like a muddy river. You could not go there tonight."

"I think I could," said the nurse, "and if you would like to earn a few gourdas, you can take me there."

Hamid nodded enthusiastically. A few gourdas were worth any amount of battling with rain and mud, and, besides, he liked Abd-el-Khader. He waited at the bottom of the stairs while the nurse went upstairs to unpack a bundle of old clothes, and while he waited his bright inquisitive eyes roamed round the premises. He had never been left alone before, and he found it very interesting. He poked his nose into the room on the left and found himself in a little kitchen with shelves on the walls and an oil stove. On one shelf stood a china basin of eggs, just low enough for him to help himself.

Hamid hesitated; he could not count, but perhaps the nurse could, and would notice if he took two. On the other hand, raw eggs sucked through a little hole in the top are delicious. Hamid had not tasted one for a long time; he thought on the whole it was worth the risk. If he waited outside the door, the nurse would never see in that rain-driven darkness; even if she noticed later she could not exactly prove it was he.

So he took one in each hand, went out into the street, and stood waiting in the dark. He did not wait long. The nurse soon appeared with a bundle and a key, and, what Hamid had not bargained for, a powerful torch. Little boys who prowl the streets at night develop cat's eyes, and do not reckon with such things.

"Come along," said the nurse, turning on her torch. "Come and get under my coat, and we can both walk in the light."

But to the nurse's surprise Hamid did not wish to walk in the light. He seemed to be taking great care to keep out of the beam, slinking along the gutters, shuffling against the wall. It was very dark and very muddy, and once or twice he slipped a little, clutching his precious eggs tightly in both hands.

"Why won't you walk with me in the middle of the road?" asked the nurse, puzzled. "You will fall if you run along in the gutter like that."

"I'm all right," muttered Hamid, rather miserably. He was not enjoying himself at all. He was so afraid of that broad beam of light, and the eggs somehow did not seem worth it. He wished he could get rid of them, and yet at the same time he wanted to hold on to them.

The light of the lamp made the surrounding darkness pitch black, and when they started climbing the steep back-alleys Hamid could not see where he was going at all. Suddenly he caught his foot on an unexpected step and fell violently forward on his face; he gave a sharp cry of shock and pain, and the nurse, who was a little ahead, turned round quickly and switched the light full on to him.

She saw him struggle to his feet, his garment covered with black mud and yellow egg-yolk. She saw his hands clasping the smashed shells, and his grazed knees streaming with blood, and she understood at once what had happened. He would have scuttled away from her, but she took hold of him quickly, and he burst into frightened tears. He had no idea what she would do. She might fetch the police and put him in prison; or she might beat him in the street. Whatever she did or did not do, she certainly would never have him in her house again. He had forfeited his right to the only shelter left to him on earth. Never again would he enter that place of warmth and light; he was shut out, and it was all his own fault.

Then through his sobs he heard the voice of the nurse speaking quietly to him.

"Come along," she said; "you've cut your knees

badly. We'll go home and bind them up, and then you can show me the way again afterward." She kept tight hold of him, and they walked home in silence, except for Hamid's sniffs. There was a lull in the rain; they entered the quiet, warm house, and she locked the door on the inside.

Still silent and ashamed, he washed his hands under the tap, and then the nurse told him to sit down. She fetched a basin of warm water and bathed his black knees till the cuts and grazes were quite clean. Then she bound them up with ointment and white bandages, and when she had finished she took a good look at him. He sat slumped in a sorry little heap covered with mud and raw egg. The only clean parts about him were the little tracks on his cheeks where his tears had made furrows through the grime.

Still without speaking she went upstairs to the bundle of old clothes and came back with a clean shirt, and a much-darned grey woolly jersey. Then she fetched more warm water and soap, and scrubbed him clean all over. Next she dressed him in his new clothes, and sat down beside him.

He looked up at her, marveling, for it was his very first experience of anyone returning good for evil, and he could not understand it. Instead of prison and a beating he had been given medicine and clean, beautiful clothes.

"Hamid," said the nurse beside him, "you fell over and hurt yourself because you would not walk in the

light with me. You were afraid to walk in the light
because you had stolen my eggs."

There was no answer.

"You don't deserve ever to come here again," went
on the nurse, "but they were my eggs and I paid for
them, so I'm going to forgive you—only you must
promise never to steal anything out of my house
again."

Hamid nodded.

"And remember," said the nurse, speaking very
slowly and earnestly, "you could not walk with me
in the light, because of your sin. The Lord Jesus says
He is the Light of the World. He asks you to walk
beside Him all the way and every day until you
reach His beautiful bright home. But first you must
tell Him about your sin, and ask Him to wash away
all its stains and make you clean, just as I washed
away the mud and the egg. Then you must leave it
behind for ever, and keep beside Him in the light."

Hamid looked down at his clean clothes and his
spotless bandage, and understood. His eggs that had
seemed so precious were gone, but he did not want
them any more. He had been forgiven and washed
and made clean. He had been brought back into
the warmth and shelter of the nurse's home. They
were going out again in the dark to find Abd-el-
Khader's house, but it would be quite different now.
He would get under the nurse's big, warm coat and

walk close beside her, sheltered from the rain; he would not stumble, and he would not be afraid of the light any longer, because he no longer had anything to hide. They would walk guided by its bright, steady beam. It would be a treat.

Half an hour later, having accomplished their errand, they returned to the house. The wind roared against the rocks behind the town, and the rain beat up the streets in cold gusts. Hamid, warm and quite comforted, popped out from under the nurse's coat, and said good-by on the step.

"But where are you going to sleep?" asked the nurse doubtfully.

"In the mosque," answered the little boy.

"But have you any blanket there?"

"No."

"Is it not very cold?"

"Tonight I shall be warm in my jersey."

"Well, you can come in tonight and sleep on the dispensary floor. The fire is still burning."

So she left him, lying comfortably on the mat, covered with a blanket, staring into the glow of the dying charcoal and thinking over the events of the evening. He had learned something that night that he would never forget all his life, and sitting up suddenly he held out his cupped hands after the Moslem fashion of prayer, and whispered the simple hymn that all Moroccan children who are taught by missionaries know by heart. They repeat the first line of each verse three times over, and the words in English go like this:

> Give me a clean heart,
>   O my Lord and my God.
>
> Take away my sins from me,
>   In the blood of my Saviour.
>
> Lead me to Heaven,
>   To Your house, O God.

CHAPTER TWELVE

A Great Gift and a Small

HAMID AND AYASHI crept shivering from the mosque one morning to find the olive groves and mountains above the town white with snow.

There were beautiful days as well as wet days; days when the sun shone, the peaks were dazzling white against powder-blue skies, and the sparkling air was crisp and cold. Those were days that whetted the children's appetites and quickened their pulses, and Hamid and Ayashi—by now fast friends—would sometimes leave the town over the crumbling back wall on the hillside and scramble up the rocks until they reached the monkeys' fortress in the mountain. They loved the screaming, chattering creatures who pelted them with stones, and they too would leap about the chatter and scream and throw stones until it was hard to tell which was boy and which was monkey.

But now the Sheep Feast, the great event of the Moorish winter, was drawing near, and the streets were thronged with fattened, frightened sheep being dragged along the cobbles with ropes, crying pitifully, and the children sat along the market walls swinging their legs and watching, and thinking it great fun. No one had ever taught them to be merciful to animals, and the struggles of these creatures doomed to die troubled them not at all. Nor did the fly-crusted sores on the flanks of pack mules, the live hens hung up for sale by their legs in the market, or the starving gutter-kittens. All these things the children saw daily, and thought nothing of them. They had received very little kindness in their young lives, so why should they give it?

The morning of the Great Feast dawned bright and clear, and the town rang with the crying of the frightened sheep being put to death in the gutters. Every rich household killed its own sheep, and the poor households shared one between several. In the market great ceremonies took place, and the high officials of town and mosque presided in their wonderful robes and turbans. For a whole week the people ate mutton served up in different ways, until they were tired of the very smell of meat, and what remained of the sheep's carcase was hung up to dry.

The beggar children enjoyed that week, for everybody was feeling generous and gave freely. Feasts were arranged for the very poor outside the water gate on the hillside, and here Hamid and Ayashi did very well indeed, flying in the face of law and order, darting from one stew to the next, never apparently moving, yet turning up everywhere. Why the Feast was being held they neither knew nor bothered to ask. Enough for them that for a whole week they ate all they wanted, and once or twice quite forgot to go to the house of the English missionary for their supper.

But when it was all over, they were glad enough to go back again, and the nurse was glad to see them. Seated cross-legged around the charcoal fire they told her all about the excitement of the past week. They described the death of the town sheep, which was carried mortally wounded on a cart drawn by galloping horses to the Moorish Government House. If the sheep died on the way it boded ill for the town, and the harvests would be poor. But the sheep, so said the boys, their faces vivid with excitement, had not died

on the way; it had outlived the journey, and therefore the town would prosper during the coming year.
They had run along beside it, part of a yelling mob,
and they had seen with their own eyes that it had
not died. And when the nurse gave a little shudder,
and asked whether the sheep had not suffered greatly,
they had shrugged their shoulders and spread out
their hands palm upward as much as to say, "We
don't know—and we don't care."

The following week was particularly cold and
bleak, and on a night of drizzling rain the children
arrived at the door as usual and knocked impatiently,
for the wind seemed to be cutting them in two, and
their sodden, fluttering rags clung to their bodies.
The door was opened at once, and they tumbled over
the threshold, eager to reach the warmth of the fireside. But once inside the passage they stood arrested
and staring, the cold and the rain forgotten.

For instead of the bright glare of electric light,
they found themselves facing the soft blaze of candles
set circle-wise on a little table in the middle of the
room, with silver boughs of olive wreathed round
them. On the floor, arranged like a picnic on a colored
cloth, a feast was spread. There were nuts, almonds,
raisins, sweets, oranges, bananas, sugar biscuits and
honey cakes, and on a tray in the corner a shining
teapot and a collection of little glasses. A kettle sang
merrily on the glowing charcoal, and the room seemed
warm with welcome. Even Kinza had stayed up to the

feast. She sat on a cushion, holding a big red and white rubber ball, her face lifted expectantly.

"It's the Feast of the Christians today," explained the nurse to the wide-eyed little boys, "so I thought we would keep it together. It is the Feast of the birth of Jesus Christ. He was the greatest gift God ever gave, so at His Feast we all give presents to each other. That is why Kinza has a rubber ball, and that is why I've bought you sweets and oranges and bananas."

The children sat down to their feast, a little awed at first by the strangeness of the silver light and their own pleasure; but gradually their tongues loosened, their toes and fingers thawed, and their cheeks flushed. They talked and ate merrily, tucking away their fruit and sweets in their rags to eat later, and sipping glass after glass of sweet, hot mint tea.

Hamid could not take his eyes off Kinza. She was dressed in her very best blue smocked frock, and her curls were brushed out. How round and sturdy she had grown! He suddenly remembered the white-faced, ragged little sister of past winters, the mud in the village, and the poverty and wretchedness. All that seemed shut out now; they seemed to be sitting cut off from the bleak world outside, in a warm kind circle of candlelight. The children were talking about feasts in general, and he began to talk too. He began telling them about the sheep feast in his own village, and the nurse, watching his eager face, felt glad.

He too had changed lately. He had never told her
what had happened to him the night he took the
eggs, but his manner was so different these days. He
was no longer a shy, hesitating little stranger; he took
his place confidently and expectantly every night,
and his whole being seemed to respond to the story
of the Saviour's love. So she sat watching him, longing
to know what had taken place in his child-heart. Suddenly her attention was caught by a little drama going
on at her side.

Kinza had risen to her feet, and there was a look on
her face the nurse had never seen before. It was a look
of dawning, half-perceived memory, as though she
had heard some dearly-loved but forgotten sound.
Then, groping a little uncertainly, feeling her way
with touch and hearing almost as sensitive as sight,
she moved toward the speaker, and stood beside him,
irresolute, tense.

At any other time Hamid would have been frightened at his secret being discovered, and would probably have pushed Kinza away. But there was an atmosphere in the room that night that cast out fear and
suspicion, and Hamid, forgetful of everyone else, put
his arm around his little sister, and drew her to him,
while she, not knowing who he was, but somehow
stirred and drawn by the voice she had once loved,
nestled up to him, and laid her shining head comfortably against his wet rags. The nurse, watching in
amazement, suddenly noticed how astonishingly alike

they were. A number of little incidents, that had seemed unimportant up to now, flashed into her mind: the almost simultaneous appearance of the two children from nowhere; Hamid's strange request to see Kinza asleep, and the secretive way he had watched her in the street. She suddenly felt quite sure that they were brother and sister; but, even if she were right, it was of no practical importance. Hamid was unlikely to betray his secret, and she on her side had no intention of parting with Kinza. She could only guess what sad misfortune had cast these two little wanderers adrift into the world, and marvel at the lovingkindness that had led them to the haven of her own home.

The other children stared too. "She knows his voice," they said wonderingly, and they too glanced at each other with surprise. But they would not speak their thoughts in front of the nurse, and soon forgot about it in further glasses of mint tea. Then, the feast being ended, the nurse made them turn round and look at a white sheet hung on the wall. She blew out the candles, and pictures appeared in the dark. The boys thought it was magic, and watched wide-eyed and open-mouthed.

It started with a picture of a girl knocking at the door of an inn, but she had to go away because there was no room. Hamid felt sorry for her, because he, too, on his first night in town, had stood and gazed into the inn, longing for shelter. He had had no

money, so he had slept on the rubbish heap, but the
woman had gone into a stable, and the next picture
showed them installed among the oxen. But a wonderful thing had happened. She was given her first-
born Son. She swaddled Him, just as his own mother
had wrapped up Kinza, and laid Him in a manger.
Kinza had had a wooden cradle, he remembered, but
this Baby was the child of very poor people, no
doubt homeless outcasts like himself.

But what was the nurse saying? The Baby in the
manger was the Lord Jesus Christ, in honor of whose
birth all Christians kept the feast of giving. He was
God's great gift, and He had come willingly. The
stable in the picture looked rather dark, lit only by
one lantern, but the home of the Son of God in
Heaven was bright with the light of glory and love.
Why had He left it?

The nurse was just telling them: "Though He was
rich, yet for your sakes He became poor." He left the
light, and came into the dark, a homeless, outcast
Child, in order to lead homeless, outcast children to
the shelter and love of His Father, God.

And now there was a third picture: there were
shepherds on the hillside keeping watch over their
flocks by night; and Hamid thought of his own
goats, and the days he had spent with them on the
mountain—but here was another picture: the Angel
of the Lord appeared, and the glory of the Lord shone
round about them. They were afraid; but apparently

the sheep were not. They seemed to be grazing quietly in the bright shelter of the Angel's wing. "Unto you is born a Saviour," said the Angel to the hillside company, and even the open heavens and the singing hosts failed to alarm the flock. Hamid suddenly remembered the anguished cries of the sheep dragged to their slaughter on the first day of the sheep feast. But the picture showed no crying and no slaughter. There was peace in Heaven and good-will on earth.

Then the last picture was flashed on the screen. The shepherds had left their flock, and here they were, barefoot, in their rough fleece coats, kneeling and worshiping at the manger. Hamid again thought of the sheep feast; the rich and the great of their land gorging themselves with fine food, and flinging what was over to the beggars and the dogs. But this was their very own feast. It was Kinza's feast, because Jesus had become a little Child, wrapped in swaddling clothes; it was his feast, because the King of Heaven had become homeless and had been lain, outcast, among the cattle. It was the feast of his own countrymen, because the shepherds had been the first to come and worship, and Mary the Baby's mother was a poor country girl. And lastly, so it seemed, it was the feast of dumb, persecuted animals, because the tired oxen, their shoulders bowed by the yoke, had drawn near to the crib, and no one had sent them away. They had all been made to feel

very close to the Child, bound together by common
links of helplessness, poverty, homelessness, and childhood.

It was over. The nurse switched on the lights, and
the pictures were gone. There was nothing visible
left of the feast but gutted candles, sweet-papers, or-
ange-peel and banana-skins. But the thought of a love
that gave, and of a love that became poor, lingered
with Hamid as he stepped out thoughtfully into the
wet street. Kinza stood in the doorway, waving to
the sound of their retreating footsteps, and as he
passed he had put out a shy hand and touched her
hair.

The other boys had gone on ahead, but Hamid
loitered along slowly, the pictures still bright in his
head, unconscious of the drizzling rain. As he passed
under a blurred street-lamp a sharp little mewing
caught his ears, and he looked down and saw a skele-
ton-like kitten, very small and wet, trying to shelter
behind a drain-pipe.

In his eleven years of life he had seen many starving kittens dying in the street, and had never given
them two seconds' thought. But tonight it was different. He could not possibly have explained, but he
had just been drawn close to a Child who was lowly
and gentle and compassionate, and all unknown to
him the first seeds of gentleness had been sown in his
heart. He found to his surprise that he cared about
the starving little creature, and he picked it up and

held it against him. It was so thin that its skin seemed
to be stretched tightly over its bones, and he could
feel its thumping heart.

What should he do with it? He had no doubts at
all. There was one open door where it would certainly
be welcome, and Kinza would probably love it. It
would be his Christmas gift to her.

He pattered back over the wet cobbles and
knocked at the nurse's door. When she opened it, he
held out the shivering, wretched creature with perfect confidence.

"It is for Kinza," he explained, "a gift of the feast.
It is very hungry and cold, so I brought it to you."

The nurse hesitated. The last thing she really
wanted just then was a half-dead ginger kitten, covered with sores and vermin, but she could not refuse,
because of what lay behind the gift. With a thrill of
joy she realized that her evening's work had not been
in vain. One little boy at least had understood, and
entered into the spirit of Christmas. He had wanted
to give, and he had been gentle and kind to an outcast kitten. It was the first time in all her experience
that she had seen a Moorish child care about the
sufferings of an animal.

So she accepted it gratefully and joyfully, and
then holding it at arm's length she carried it to a box
near the fire and sprinkled it all over with disinfect-
ant powder. Then she gave it a saucer of milk, and it
twitched its tail at an impertinent angle, and lapped

it up—a tough, gallant little kitten, unconquered by adversity! It deserved to be saved.

As she sat watching it she had a sudden vision, which passed swiftly and left her laughing. She thought she saw all the Christmas love-gifts of all the ages heaped together before the manger—the gold, the frankincense, the myrrh; the stars, the homage of heaven, the treasure and worship of earth. And perched on top of the glittering pile, precious in the eyes of the One to whom it was given, was a thin, flea-ridden, ginger kitten, with its tail at an impertinent angle—the first-fruits of a little boy's compassion.

PART TWO

CHAPTER THIRTEEN

Jenny Must Have Sunshine

MANY, MANY MILES AWAY, under different Christ-mas stars, another party was in progress. It had this much in common with the party in the Nurse's house—the children at each were radiantly, gloriously happy.

Otherwise it was a quite different kind of party. Instead of oranges and nuts and sweets there were jellies and trifles and chocolate biscuits, and a big Christmas cake; and instead of black, wet rags there were bright-colored dresses and jerseys, and the girls had gay ribbons in their hair. It should have been a perfect party, and yet when the tea and games were over, and the joyful children gathered under the Christmas tree to sing carols, the grown-up visitors all felt sad, and one small visitor of nine years old felt saddest of all.

For this was a Blind School, and the little singers with their bright faces lit up by the candles could not see the tree or the soft lanterns or the toys they had been given. They had eaten their meal with enormous relish, and danced merrily up and down to the sound of music, and now they were singing with all their hearts and souls; and Jenny, sitting with her mother and father in the audience, found she had a lump in her throat. If she always had to live in the dark she was quite certain she would never be happy again. She shut her eyes for a moment, and tried to imagine what it would be like to be blind, but it was really too dreadful even to think about, so she opened them again quickly, and watched the children.

They were singing a carol now—one that Jenny herself had learned at school:

> Star of wonder, star of light,
>   Star with royal beauty bright,
> Westward leading, still proceeding,
>   Guide us to thy perfect Light.

And Jenny, who was a practical child, wondered why

they had been taught such words. What was the good of singing about perfect light when they were doomed to spend all their days in darkness? Yet, as she watched them, she had to own to herself that not one little singer looked unhappy; the lifted shining faces seemed almost as though they had caught sight of that Christmas star, and the perfect Light beyond it—very far away, but clear in the distance.

Jenny knew the story of that carol, and when they had decorated the room at her school for the Christmas party they had made a beautiful model frieze, sticking the figures on dark blue paper to represent a night sky. They had all helped to color and cut out the figures, and their teacher had stuck them on one by one: three lurching camels with bright trappings, and three wise men with long white beards and beautiful flasks and caskets of treasures—the gold, the frankincense and the myrrh; a shining star up above, beaming down on a humble little house where a lowly woman sat playing with her baby Boy who was, in some strange way that Jenny could not understand, the perfect Light toward which they were traveling.

Her mother touched her, because the carols were over and everyone was clapping—except for Jenny, whose thoughts were far away. She came back to earth with a start, and began clapping very loudly, so that the blind children should see how pleased she was, until her mother signed to her to stop because someone wanted to make a speech. And then it was all over, and the children crowded around to say good-by, touching and feeling and chattering, and the "littlest ones" were borne away happy and sleepy to bed. But the bigger ones thronged the doorway to wave and shout to the sound of the cars driving away; and that was the last Jenny saw of them—a mass of rosy, laughing faces and waving hands.

She was very quiet on the way home, and her mother, thinking she was tired, hurried her up to her room, lit a gas fire, and bustled her into bed. Jenny had been ill, and this was her first real outing for three months. Her mother had wondered whether she ought to go, but Jenny had insisted, and as usual had got her way. Her father had recently joined the Council of the Blind School and they had all been invited to the Christmas party.

She nestled down under her pink satin eiderdown and surveyed her beautiful array of Christmas presents—the books, the games, the cosy new dressing gown, the little gold wrist watch and the traveling case. It had been a very satisfactory Christmas, and the best present of all—a pony of her very own—was down in the stable. For the first time in her rather self-centered little life it suddenly occurred to Jenny, as she lay waiting for her mother to bring her good-night drink, that she was really a very fortunate child. She thought of the blind children with the toys they could not see, and the children out in Morocco who had no toys at all and, often, no food. Her Aunt Rosemary looked after some of them, and had written her an early Christmas letter all about them, and Jenny had been thrilled. It had been like a new, exciting story, giving her a peep into a world she knew nothing about, a world where children went about in rags, and earned their own living, and slept by themselves out of doors—a world where little babies got ill because they had not enough to eat. Jenny adored babies, but the only babies she had ever met at close quarters were defended by nurses in uniform, and she had not been allowed to hold them in her arms as she had longed to do. These other babies were probably too poor to have nurses, and there was a chance that she would be allowed to pick them up.

For the wonderful thing was that in a very short time Jenny would actually see the children that Auntie Rosemary had written about; only six weeks after Christmas she and her father and mother were to set out by car on the long journey that would finish up with a visit to Auntie Rosemary and her beggar-children in the mountains of North Africa.

They were setting out in search of sunshine, for the doctor had said that Jenny needed sunshine—and therefore sunshine she must have. Tonics, medicines, cream, drives in the car—all these she had had in plenty; but neither love nor money could procure sunshine in England in January, so southward they were going to a land of blue skies and yellow beaches and calm seas, where she would grow strong and brown

and sturdy. To Jenny it seemed a magic journey. She
felt one in spirit with swallows which had skimmed
away from grey skies and storms and cold rain, southward, southward, southward, guided by some sure
instinct to journey toward the light, until one fair
morning they flew into a world of sunshine on wings
tipped with gold and silver.

She wondered how her father would know the way,
and supposed they would just follow the sun, as the
Wise Men had followed the star. She was feeling
rather sleepy and had quite forgotten about the road
maps. Stars, sunshine, Christmas trees, swallows with
bright-tipped wings—they all merged into a golden
dream, and when her mother returned with a drink
and sugar biscuits on a tray decorated with mistletoe
she found her little daughter fast asleep. She stood
looking down on the flushed face and tumbled hair
for a moment, and then put out the light, opened the
big window, and slipped away, leaving Jenny to
dream, and to breathe in quiet healing draughts of
fresh air and starry winds.

Six weeks later the car was in truth speeding southward, and Jenny, in a nest of rugs and warm wraps,
sat enthroned in the back. They had all been sea-
sick crossing the Channel, which was horrible, but
once the grey heaving waters had been left behind,
and they were well and truly off, skimming along the
straight French roads between miles of poplars, the

fun began. It was fascinating to hear the people talking a different language, and to drive through cobbled villages where pinafored children trotted along the streets carrying loaves of bread a couple of feet long under their arms. They stopped in some of the cathedral towns and visited the old churches, and even Jenny's chatter was awed into silence by the beauty of the stained glass windows in the Cathedral at Chartres. She stayed behind by the font looking up at the colors, unfaded by the passage of centuries, gold and crimson and sapphire, as fresh as on the day when the craftsman dedicated his skill to the light of the glory of God. And as she stood looking, the sun beamed out from behind a cloud, and she found herself standing in a rainbow of reflected color, with a pavement of delicate tints set under her feet. She could see her own hair shining like burnished gold on her shoulder, and her blue dress was bright as the virgin's gown in the window above. The rest of the Cathedral was dim and cool, but she was standing all alone in an island of light, bathed in glory and color. "Guide us to thy Perfect Light," she said to herself, half carried away by the wonderful experience. But even as the words flashed through her mind another cloud passed across the sun, and the stones on which she stood and her own little person all looked quite ordinary again. Nothing had changed at all; only for a moment she and all around her had been transformed by the sunlight, gathered up and mirrored and breaking over her in the colors of the glass.

On the fourth day they crossed the borders into Spain and began climbing the Basque mountains, deep in snow. They crossed the high pass in an exciting blizzard, and stopped for the night at a little hotel halfway down on the other side. Here, gathered round a blazing fire, they ate big thick potato omelettes and fried onions and olives; and Jenny, warm and glowing and full of food, could scarcely stumble up to bed for sleep. Her mother tucked her into her wooden bed, and left her dreaming.

She woke very early in the morning because the cocks in the yard below were making such a noise. It was still quite dark, but she jumped out of bed, flung open the window, and looked out into the frosty air. Cold and white and beautiful rose the mountains, and the first streaks of dawn glimmered behind them, while above them hung the morning star. Jenny had never seen such a big, bright star before. She jumped back into bed because it was so cold, but lay with her head resting on her arms, looking at it, and watching the paling skies. Perhaps this was the star that the Wise Men had followed, traveling all night, their weary eyes uplifted toward it until sunrise eclipsed its shining. Again the faces of the blind children flashed into her mind, and the cadence of their song:

> Star of wonder, star of light,
> Guide us to thy Perfect Light.

She suddenly wished that she and her mother and
father were lurching over the white mountains on
three camels instead of in the automobile, their eyes
fixed on the star, their luggage packed in jeweled caskets, seeking perfect light. What would the end of
their journey be? she wondered, and where would
perfect light be found? In the far land of sunshine to
which the swallows had flown, or at the feet of a
Baby? She did not know, and she fell asleep again
for a couple of hours. When she woke, the snowy
mountains were sparkling against a blue sky, and her
mother was standing over her with breakfast on a
tray.

"Darling," she said, "we've left you to the last
minute. Eat this up, and get dressed. Daddy's champ-
ing by the car. He says we ought to get to Madrid by
this evening."

CHAPTER FOURTEEN

The Guests Arrive

VERY EARLY one morning in March, the English nurse woke, got out of bed at once, and ran up to her flat roof to look at the weather. It was going to be a fine day, she decided, for the eastern sky was fleeced all over with feathery, pink sunrise clouds, and the west was clear as crystal. And this was just as it should be, thought the nurse happily to herself, for this was the day she had looked forward to for so long. Her cousin from England, with whom she had lived as a child, was arriving to stay in the hotel for a fortnight. Her husband was coming with her, and they were bringing Jenny.

It was the thought of Jenny that made the English nurse sing as she got breakfast and woke Kinza, who was lying in a ball on a mattress on the floor, her ginger kitten close beside her. Kinza's first action on waking was always to stretch out her hand and make sure that the ginger kitten was where it should be, and if by any chance it had gone for a walk a commotion followed. But this morning all was well, and she sat up, drew her pet into her lap, and began to sing, too, loudly, tunelessly and timelessly; it was her way of announcing that she was ready to be washed and dressed in preparation for another happy day.

The English nurse, hearing the signal, came down from the roof and attended to Kinza. Then hand in hand they climbed the stairs and set themselves breakfast at a low, round table under a blue spring sky. The nurse sat on a stool, and Kinza and the kitten sat on a mat. The coffee was fragrant and piping hot, the kitten's milk was creamy, and each was perfectly satisfied with the present company. A happier trio could not have been found anywhere, and as Kinza buried her face in her bowl the sun came up over the roof gable and shone warm on her curls.

"The little girl is coming today," announced the nurse, as she tidied up and did her best not to trip over Kinza and the kitten, who were having a complicated game with a ball, and kept landing between her feet. "We are going to take a holiday. We will go to the market together and buy nice things to eat, and then we'll make a feast for the little girl."

"A feast, a feast!" shouted Kinza, capering about like a clumsy little kid, and falling over the waste paper basket. "I will carry the basket for you. Let's go now."

"Yes, let's," said the nurse, and off they went into the sunshine hand in hand. She had not taken a weekday holiday for a long time; she usually stayed in in the morning. But today she had told the people not to come; she was going to be free to make ready for Jenny, and now while the day was still fresh and young she was going to climb up to the hillside behind the town and pick flowers.

It was too far for Kinza, so when they had done their shopping she left baby and basket on the step of the doughnut shop in the charge of Hamid. She often did this when she was busy, for she felt quite sure that the two children were connected—probably brother and sister—and had a right to each other's company. Kinza was always perfectly safe and happy when Hamid looked after her, although she sometimes ended up a little greasy, and not very keen on her dinner. She was very fond of doughnuts, and would eat all that were offered her.

Once by herself, the nurse almost ran up the steep, cobbled streets, past the tumbledown shacks on the outskirts of the town, with their evil-smelling rubbish-heaps, and out through the gate in the ruined wall that led on to the hillside. As she climbed, a clean warm wind came swooping to meet her, and the sun shone full on her lifted face. Still half-running, she reached the flat summit of the first little hill, which terraced the mountain behind. She turned to look at the steep town below her and the green watered valley beyond. She stood gazing at the sloping tiers of roofs with their curved, lichened tiles, and the white towers of the several mosques lifting their bright crescents over the city. Then she picked out her own little home in the back street above the market, and realized with a thrill of humble joy that the Lord Jesus had at least one witness in that sin-shadowed place. She thought of the Good Shepherd seeking His lost sheep among these mountains where villages clustered on the ledges, and in the narrow streets of the little town. Here and there, she believed, were those who had heard His voice—two or three frightened, illiterate women, a few ignorant, ragged children, precious little lights in that vast darkness; but hers was the only home where His presence was openly loved. "The Son of Man hath not where to lay His

head," He had once said wearily, and in the town below her all doors were closed to Him except hers—
she would not have changed her little home for any
palace in the world, or her work for any other.

She suddenly forgot she would soon be middle-
aged and felt very young indeed. Singing for joy she
jumped down from the rock on which she was standing and began picking flowers. They were growing
all round her, for it was high tide of spring, and she
gathered fragrant white narcissi, small blue irises and
crimson lilies. "How beautiful they are!" she cried
aloud. "I shall bring Jenny up here, and we'll pick
them together."

Her thoughts went back to Jenny, and she began
to feel some misgivings. Jenny was the daughter of
Elizabeth, the cousin whose company had so cheered
her lonely orphaned childhood, but she and her
cousin had drifted apart since they had grown up.
Their fortunes, their tastes, their interests were so
different. Their love for Jenny seemed the only link
left between them.

They had been like sisters once, but Elizabeth had
married a rich man, and had gone to live in his beautiful home; here Jenny had been brought up, surrounded by beauty and peace, possessing all that love
and money could give. They would gladly have made
a home for Aunt Rosemary, too, but she, during her
hospital training, had also come face to face with
One who loved her, and He had sent her out to the

little town in the mountains to seek for His lost sheep and lambs. The whole affair had seemed quite foolish to Elizabeth and her husband.

Knowing how mad it seemed to them, Rosemary had found it difficult to write about the little joys and sorrows of her lonely mission station, just as Elizabeth found it difficult to write about the happy fullness of her married life; so their occasional letters were chiefly about Jenny, and every Christmas Rosemary received a new photograph. She had kept them all in a little album, starting with a bald, round-eyed baby, who within a year had turned into a toddler in woolly leggings, staggering along with curls tumbling over her eyes. Then came Jenny in rompers on the beach, Jenny waist-high in a field of daisies, Jenny in an apron bathing her dolls. After that the years seemed to fly, and Rosemary got quite a shock one Christmas when she received a photograph of Jenny with her curls tied neatly back with a ribbon, setting off to school in a blazer and gym tunic.

The last one showed Jenny mounted on a pony, and it was the thought of the pony that produced the misgivings in Aunt Rosemary's mind. How foolish it was of her to build such high hopes on the child's visit! What had she to offer a little girl who had been used to riding a pony on her father's estate, and who was the owner of a dream-nursery, where china dolls as big as babies lay in proper cots under satin eiderdowns? Jenny had once told her about them in a let-

ter. She would probably be bored with the little
entertainments that sent Moorish children into rap-
tures. Aunt Rosemary, feeling a little downcast, hurried back down the mountain with her flowers, collected a happy, sticky Kinza, and went home.

She went to the toy-cupboard and inspected it
rather sadly. There were some thumbed, dog-eared
scrapbooks, some faded puzzles and chipped bricks,
some common little dolls and a box of stubby chalks.
All had been so obviously used and loved and kissed
and clutched and exulted over by children who had
never seen toys before, and they were all so shabby.
Aunt Rosemary shut the cupboard with a sigh, and
went to the kitchen to make buns.

By half-past four the little house was as bright as
scrubbing and polishing could make it, and the sitting-room was sweet with the scent of wild narcissi.
Tea was laid ready, the kettle was singing on the
stove, and Aunt Rosemary and Kinza went forth to
meet the car in front of the hotel.

It arrived punctually, a smart, streamlined vehicle,
and the little boys surged round, fighting each other
in their efforts to carry in the luggage. Aunt Rosemary stood waiting for them to alight, and above the
pandemonium she heard a clear child's voice cry out,
"Oh, Mummy, look! what a sweet little girl! you never
told me Auntie Rosemary had a little girl."

And then next moment they had extricated themselves from the mob of little boys, and Elizabeth,

looking just as young as she had looked ten years before, was kissing her cousin warmly. Jenny, a child of one idea, was squatting on the ground, trying to make friends with Kinza.

"Jenny," said her mother, reprovingly, "you haven't greeted Auntie Rosemary."

Jenny got up, kissed her aunt politely and turned her attention back to Kinza. The two women left them for a moment, in order to talk to Jenny's father, who was arranging about the luggage and the hotel, and, while passports were produced and forms filled in, Aunt Rosemary stood quietly watching the child, whom for ten whole years she had longed to see.

She saw a slender, long-legged little girl in a beautiful blue smocked dress and white sandals; bright hair curling loosely to her shoulders, and big grey eyes set in an eager brown face with a pointed little chin; an elfin-looking child, thought Aunt Rosemary to herself, and went over to make friends.

Jenny turned a troubled face to her aunt.

"What is the matter with this little girl?" she asked wonderingly. "I showed her my pretty brooch, and she just stares in front of her."

"I'm afraid she's blind, Jenny," said Aunt Rosemary gently. "But it doesn't mean you can't play with her. You must give her toys she can feel, and you must sing to her, and let her touch you. She'll soon love you."

She lifted Kinza's tiny hand and passed it lightly

over Jenny's face and hair. "That's how she gets to
know people," she explained, and then turned to
speak to Mr. and Mrs. Swift, who had just arrived.
But before she could say anything Jenny had seized
her mother's hand and was looking up at her, her
grey eyes brimming with tears.

"She's blind, Mummy," she whispered, "like the
little Christmas children."

"Never mind," replied Mrs. Swift gently. "She
looks a very happy little girl, and we must find her a
little present. Now let's come and see Auntie Rosemary's house."

They set off across the market, the grown-ups walking ahead, and Jenny leading Kinza, too taken up
with her new playmate to notice much of the town
about her. She was happier than she had been all the
holiday, for, much as she loved her mother and father,
she was only ten, and she longed for other children
to play with; most of all she longed for something to
look after. She was too old for dolls; her pets had all
been left at home, and she missed them dreadfully.
But a curly-haired, blind baby of three was far better
than pets; she had never dreamed of anything so exciting.

They had reached the narrow back street where
Auntie Rosemary lived, and Mrs. Swift was talking
in rather a strained voice, and trying not to look horrified at the babies sitting on the cobbles, and the
amazing ragged old beggar chanting in one of the

doorways. Then she suddenly looked very horrified indeed, for Auntie Rosemary had stopped in front of the last house, and was drawing out her key; on the doorstep, barring the entrance, sat a very poor woman holding something to her breast, under her rags.

Rosemary spoke to the woman, who drew aside her rags and held out a baby, all skin and bones, half-dead with sickness and exhaustion. Mrs. Swift put out her hand to take hold of Jenny, but she was too late; her child had stepped forward, and both she and Aunt Rosemary were stooping over the pathetic little creature, quite absorbed.

"Jenny!" commanded her mother, "come here." But Jenny took not the slightest notice. She turned tragic eyes to her aunt.

"Is it going to die?" she whispered.

"I don't know; I hope not," replied Aunt Rosemary. "Come in."

She opened the front door, led the woman into the dispensary, and told her to sit down while she turned back to her guests. Mrs. Swift was standing very still, almost as though she had forgotten where she was, for, having got over her first shock of horror at finding such a wretched creature on Rosemary's doorstep, she had noticed the woman's face—a young, patient face, resigned to suffering, with beautiful dark eyes that gleamed with hope as she lifted her baby toward the nurse. Mrs. Swift suddenly remembered how she had once sat nursing Jenny in her arms: when you

stripped away the outer trappings there was not so
very much difference between them—just another
mother holding another child. What was this woman
really feeling like under that still mask of her resig-
nation? Mrs. Swift turned to her cousin.

"Rosemary," she urged, "don't mind about us; we
can look after ourselves. You go and see to that poor
baby."

Aunt Rosemary hestitated. "Well, come upstairs,"
she said, "and I can show you where the sitting-room
is. Tea is all ready, and the kettle is boiling."

It was a surprise to enter a house in that dingy
street and find it bright with pictures and flowers,
and a delicious meal set out on pretty china. Aunt
Rosemary, after taking them to her bedroom, sat them
down on the low mattress seats, and made tea. Then
she spoke rather shyly.

"It seems awfully rude," she said, "but would you
mind if I left you just for ten minutes? You see, I
know this woman; she's lost four babies—this one is
all she's got."

Jenny slipped her hand into her aunt's.

"I'm coming to help you," she announced.

"No, Jenny," exclaimed her mother firmly; "it's
quite out of the question. Come and sit down and
have your tea."

Jenny flew into a passion at once.

"I want to go!" she stormed; "I want to see that
baby get well. I don't want any tea! Say I can come,

Auntie Rosemary; it's your house. Daddy, say I can go. Mummy, you might let me . . ."

Her father most unexpectedly came to Jenny's rescue.

"What is the matter with that baby?" he asked. "Has it got anything infectious?"

"I shouldn't think so," answered Aunt Rosemary. "I've seen it before; it's suffering from starvation and wrong feeding."

"Then, Elizabeth, I should let her go, if Rosemary doesn't mind," said Mr. Swift; and, as Jenny left the room triumphantly, he turned to his wife.

"Darling," he said, "let her help all she can. She needs to help someone. It may make her less self-centered to see that sort of thing, and I'm sure Rosemary will be sensible about infection."

"Perhaps so," agreed Jenny's mother, and she gave a little sigh. "If only she could have had younger brothers and sisters," she added wistfully.

Meanwhile Jenny and her aunt were bending over the white-faced baby, and the mother was recounting its pitiful history—the usual tale of poverty, ignorance, and wrong feeding. It seemed almost too late to help, but perhaps there was still a chance. Aunt Rosemary, nursing the tiny thing in the dispensary blanket, turned to Jenny.

"Go upstairs, Jenny," she said, "and bring me a cup and a spoon and some sugar from the shelf above the stove."

Jenny obeyed, moving swiftly and lightly.

"And now go and fetch the kettle," commanded her aunt.

Jenny was off in a flash.

"Now bring me those white tablets on the third shelf over there," went on her aunt, speaking very gravely; and Jenny began to feel rather uncomfortable. She was used to being admired by everyone, but she had an uncomfortable feeling that her aunt thoroughly disapproved of her.

"Now, please, rinse out the cup and spoon with some of that boiled water . . . now crush up one tablet . . . mix it with a very little water . . . pass me that bottle . . . "

Jenny forgot her temper, forgot her aunt, and forgot herself. She knelt perfectly still on the mat, only conscious of the weak little gurgling sound as the baby tried to swallow. Almost drop by drop the medicine disappeared and the baby was not sick. It took a few more spoonfuls of sweetened water, and then Aunt Rosemary began talking to the mother in Arabic, explaining that she must sit quietly for an hour and then they would give the child another drink.

"It must get better," murmured Jenny to herself. "It must! it must!"

And then Aunt Rosemary did something that surprised Jenny, who had never seen anyone do such a thing before, except in a church. She pointed to the picture of Jesus holding a child in His arms, and told the woman all about it, and then laying her hand on the woman's knees she prayed aloud for the little sick baby. Jenny could not understand what her aunt was saying, but she knew she was praying, because her eyes were closed.

"I wonder if that really does any good," thought Jenny to herself, and she too glanced up at the painting on the wall, and somehow the sight of the pictured child, so closely held, made the real baby seem safer.

"It's sure to get better," breathed Jenny to herself, bending over it again. And as she watched, the eyelids fluttered, and the baby opened its eyes.

CHAPTER FIFTEEN

"Ask Him to Let It Be Yes"

AFTER THAT, no further plans were needed, for Jenny announced firmly that they were going to remain in the town until it was time to go home to England and she was going to be Kinza's nurse and help Aunt Rosemary every day with the sick babies in the dispensary.

Mr. Swift laughed comfortably and then wondered

what he was going to do with himself, stuck fast in an
out-of-the-way mountain village for three weeks, in
order to satisfy his daughter's sudden liking for sick
babies. Mrs. Swift sighed anxiously and insisted that
Jenny should gargle three times a day. Jenny herself was openly thrilled, and Aunt Rosemary was
secretly very happy. From their point of view the
holiday was being a complete success.

It was Sunday afternoon, and on Sunday no one
came to the dispensary. There had been a meeting for
women in the afternoon. Jenny had arrived just as
they were leaving, and had watched them go slowly
down the street, their babies tied tightly on their
backs, and the white outer garment that covered them
from head to toe thrown on top.

"They look like camels with humps, carrying their
babies like that," remarked Jenny, entering the house
with a hop and skip. "You'd think their babies would
be suffocated, wouldn't you? Why don't they have
baby carriages like ordinary people?"

"They couldn't afford to buy them," replied Aunt
Rosemary, smiling, "but it certainly isn't a very good
way to carry them. A lot of the babies grow up with
weak chests through lack of fresh air. You've noticed
how pale some of them look."

"And spotty and thin and dirty," added Jenny
wrinkling her small nose. "It's a pity there aren't
more people like you to teach them how to look after
their babies properly. You know, Auntie, I've been

thinking, and I've decided that when I grow up I'm going to be a missionary, too, and I'm going to come out here, and have a dispensary and make all the ill people better like you do. I think it's such fun."

Aunt Rosemary looked down into the brown, confident little face lifted to hers, and she didn't answer for a moment or two.

"You couldn't be a missionary unless a very important thing happened to you first, Jenny," she said at last.

"Why not, Auntie?" inquired Jenny, surprised. "I could learn to be a nurse and how to look after babies. I wouldn't need to know anything else, would I?"

"Yes, I think you would," replied Aunt Rosemary with a little smile, "but I'm not going to tell you just here in the hall. Let's take some sandwiches, and go and have tea in the tower gardens, and then we can talk about it. Kinza will be awake by now, and she loves the tower gardens."

"Oo, lovely!" cried Jenny and went up the stairs two steps at a time to make preparations. "Mummy said I could stay to tea if you happened to invite me. I specially asked her."

"That was very foreseeing of you," said Aunt Rosemary, laughing. "Would you like to get Kinza ready while I collect the tea? The kettle will be boiling already, so we can go almost at once."

Ten minutes later Aunt Rosemary, Jenny and Kinza were making their way across the sleepy market

square to the old crumbling gate in the wall of the
tower. Jenny carried the basket, and Kinza carried
her ball. They were chattering gaily as they climbed
the steps, but as they entered the retreat of the tower
garden a silence fell over them, because it was so
beautiful, and Kinza stood still and sniffed appreci-
atively. They seemed to be walled in, not by brick
or stone, but by great swaying curtains of wistaria
and jasmine, and the beds were bright with wall-
flowers and narcissi. Sunshine streamed over everything, distilling the perfume of the flowers, and the
silence was broken only by the busy rattle of the
storks nesting, the occasional hoarse cry of the peacock, and a soft splashing in the pond where a white
goose was teaching seven fluffy goslings to swim.

"Don't let Kinza fall in," warned Aunt Rosemary.
"You just hang on to her while I spread out the tea."

She unpacked the basket and then sat for a few moments quietly watching the two children at play.
Kinza was growing into a beautiful little girl now,
strong and sturdy, with rounded limbs and soft dark
curls. Who was she, and what would become of her?
It was time some practical plan was made about her
future, thought Aunt Rosemary to herself, if she
was to grow up useful and clever with her hands. And
Jenny, standing under the trailing jasmine, poised to
run, lithe and free as a bird, what would become of
her? Was she going to grow up careless, self-centered,
self-satisfied? "I needn't know anything else, need

I?" she had said lightly half an hour ago: her whole future lay in the answer.

Jenny caught sight of the spread tea and, taking Kanża's hand in hers, came running up. They were sitting on a low wall by the pond in the very center of the garden, beneath an arch covered with little green shoots that would soon break out into a mass of rambler roses. Kinza was instantly absorbed in a bun, and Jenny, having helped herself to a sandwich, turned her questioning face to her aunt.

"What else would I have to know to be a missionary?" she asked, as though the conversation had never left off.

"It depends on what you want to do," replied Aunt Rosemary steadily. "If you simply want to heal their illnesses, then you must just train to be a nurse or a doctor. But most of them are so poor that they will probably get ill again very quickly, and in any case none of our bodies last very long. The part of them that really matters is the part that is going to last for ever, their real selves that we call their spirits. You can only really help them and make them happy by leading them to the Lord Jesus, and you can't possibly show the Lord Jesus to anyone else unless you've seen Him yourself. So it isn't really a matter of *what* you know at all, but *whom* you know."

"But you spend ever such a long time every day giving them medicine," said Jenny. "Why couldn't I just do that?"

"You could," said Aunt Rosemary. "But, you see, you don't understand why I spend a long time giving medicines, and I'm going to explain to you. All these poor people are sinful, and only Jesus can forgive them; all of them are afraid of death, and only Jesus can take away their fear; most of them are sad and tired, and only Jesus can comfort them and give them rest. And He longs to reach them with His forgiveness and His love, but because He isn't on earth any more they can't see Him or hear Him as they did in Bible days. So He enters into the hearts of people who love Him, and He uses their lips to speak, and He uses their hands to touch. And I don't just give them medicine to make them better, much as I like to cure their illnesses. I give it because I want them to see that Jesus in me cares about their pain, and wants to help them. It's no good just *talking* about the love of Jesus; they don't understand. You have to *show* it to them by loving deeds. But the first thing you have to be sure of is that Jesus is actually there, loving in you and through you. Otherwise it's just like taking an empty lantern out in the dark."

Jenny was silent.

"Well, how do you know if He's there or not?" she asked curiously.

"How does the light get into the empty lantern?" asked Aunt Rosemary. "It's just a matter of opening a door, and placing a candle inside. Jesus is the Light, and He wants to come in; and we, by believing,

open the door and ask Him in. Then, if the glass of
the lantern is clean, the light shines out clearly; but
if the glass is clouded and dirty the light will be very
dim. So the first thing Jesus does with His light is to
show us the sins that are going to hide Him—the
tempers, self-will, impatience, and disobedience.
Then, if we really want Him to, He makes us clean,
and His beautiful clear beams of love shine out
through us; and people lost and afraid in the dark
come flocking to the light. But they don't think about
the lantern at all—it's the light they want. Missionaries are really very unimportant people. They are
just empty lanterns. It's the light that matters."

There was another pause.

"So I suppose only very good people can be missionaries," Jenny said thoughtfully.

"It's not exactly that," said Aunt Rosemary. "Many
people are very good and kind without Jesus, just as
gilded lanterns shine if you put them in the sun—but
in the evening the sun sets. And our own goodness
unfortunately lasts only just as long as we do—until
we die. The love and life and goodness of Jesus last
forever, and the person in whom His light is burning will last forever as well. It is what is called eternal
life; and, of course, it's a far better, stronger, whiter
sort of goodness than the other kind. It is perfect
goodness, and no one except Jesus has ever been perfectly good."

"There are Mummy and Daddy coming into the

garden," exclaimed Jenny suddenly, and she jumped up and sped along the little paths toward them, bright curls flying in the warm breeze. She was rather glad to escape from this conversation, for Auntie Rosemary was saying some quite disturbing things, and Jenny did not really like being disturbed—that bit about missionaries being unimportant, for instance. She had always been by far the most important person in the small circle in which she had lived; the lives of her mother and father and nurse, and the activities of the servants, had always centered in her well-being and wishes. Even at school she knew herself to be a person of importance, and the other children thought it an honor to be invited to her house. And very right and proper too, thought Jenny, landing with a skip in her father's arms; the smile on his face and the look in her mother's eyes reassured her at once. Whatever happened, she would always be by far the most important person in the world to her mother and father.

Auntie Rosemary followed, leading a rather crumb-covered Kinza, and her eyes met Elizabeth's over Jenny's head, happy because it was still so wonderful to see Jenny running about and strong again. One of the best parts of the holiday to both women had been the renewal of their old friendship, which now blossomed as strong and sure as it had done before their very different ways of life had seemed to separate them. Elizabeth's charm and kindness and the serenity of her married life drew out Rosemary's admiration.

Elizabeth, on her side, had come to admit that her
cousin was not altogether wasting her time. The look
on the face of the sick baby's mother had taught her
that, and in spite of the germs and sores of the dispensary she trusted Rosemary with Jenny as she had never
trusted anyone before. And this was strange, for a few
weeks ago she, who had always been so careful to sur-
round her little girl with sunshine and beauty, would
have been horrified at Jenny's having anything to do
with poverty and illness.

But there are different sorts of beauty, she had
thought to herself. Healing and helping and loving
and giving are beautiful. I don't want Jenny to be a
recluse, or anything like that. I want her to get on
in the world and marry well—but I want her to
grow up good and unselfish, too, and I think Rosemary can help her in that way.

When she had voiced her thoughts to her husband
he had agreed. "She's learning something practical in
that dispensary," he said, "and she may find she's
cut out for nursing. They don't seem to think at
school that she's overburdened with brains, and if
war comes later she'll have to do something like
everyone else."

Whereupon Jenny's mother had shuddered and
changed the subject. Jenny and war did not seem
to her to fit at all; she disliked their being mentioned
in the same breath.

"Rosemary," said Elizabeth, nestling Kinza against

her, "couldn't you desert your little brats just for once this evening, and come and have supper with us at the hotel?"

"They don't come on Sunday," replied Rosemary. "It's my day off, except for the afternoon meeting. I'd love to come. I'll go home and get Kinza safely to sleep, and then I'll be along."

"Oh, Mummy, look!" cried Jenny. "The peacock has opened his tail." And she hurried her parents off to see, while Rosemary and Kinza made their way home, the low sun sending long, bright, mellow rays across the market square. It was quite early, and she left Kinza to play in a patch of sunlight on the doorstep; the other babies who lived in the street came waddling up solemnly and sat down beside her. Rosemary gave them a lump of plasticine, and they all began to make plasticine apples, rolling small pieces round and round in their fat hands. Such funny little figures they looked, the baby girls dressed in long bunchy skirts like their mothers, and the baby boys, like little old men, in dark homespun gowns and hoods. They worked quietly, absorbed, for some time, then suddenly the silence was broken by delighted peals of joyous baby laughter, and Rosemary went down to find that a portly gentleman of three had been very, very original and made a banana. Kinza, who could not possibly have known what it was all about, was laughing louder than anyone else.

Rosemary squatted on the step beside them and

admired their works of art, and they beamed and
cuddled up to her and asked for pictures. They were
well-to-do babies, on the whole, and the two little
girls wore silver bands slung round their necks as
protecting charms. Their names meant Orangeblos-
som and Angel. The three little boys looked at her
with bright mischievous eyes, and laid sticky paws
on her knee. Their names meant Servant of the
Prophet, Glory of Religion, and My Lord of Arabia.
One day their names would suit them, and they would
turn into proud, arrogant Moslems like their fathers,
but just at the moment they looked more like a family
of kittens.

Rosemary showed them a picture of a little lost
lamb saying "maa-maa" on the mountain, and the
babies laughed and said "maa-maa," too. Then the
Shepherd came and carried the little lamb home on
His shoulders rejoicing, and its mother said "baa-baa."
The babies had often heard this story before, but they
did not mind a bit. It never grew any less exciting,
and when Rosemary finally carried Kinza off to bed,
they were still sitting on the step saying "baa-baa."
Kinza, washed and undressed, knelt on her little mat
to say her prayers. "Thank You for my happy day,
and because we had tea in the garden, and bless
Jenny and all the babies in the street," prayed Kinza
hurriedly, but she was not really thinking about the
babies. It was Sunday night, and on Sunday night
she always had a sweet in bed and she thought of

nothing else for a long time beforehand. It was Rosemary who thought of the babies in the street—poor little lost lambs, squatting in the twilight in front of an open door, saying "baa"!

An hour later she was sitting in the big hotel dining room, under a cut glass chandelier, eating a four course dinner with Mr. and Mrs. Swift and Jenny, who had all dressed up in their very best to welcome her. It was a great treat to Rosemary to come out to supper, and there was always so much to say when she and Elizabeth got together. Tonight the talk turned upon Kinza.

"She's such a beautiful little creature," said Mrs. Swift; "it seems so cruel she should be blind. What do you propose to do with her in the future, Rosemary?"

"I would like her to go to some training school in about three years' time," said Rosemary, "where she can learn Braille and basket-work. She could earn her own living like that out here, and when she was really proficient she could come back to me. A blind girl who was a true Christian could be a missionary to her own people later on."

Jenny leaned forward across the table, nearly upsetting her glass in her eagerness.

"The Blind School, Daddy!" she cried, "where they invited us all at Christmas. If Kinza went there, Mummy, she could come and stay with us sometimes; and I'd look after her; it would be like having a little sister, and I'd see her lots and lots, and she'd be so happy if I was there; and they had such a lovely time at Christmas. Oh, when can she come, Auntie Rosemary? couldn't we take her home with us this time?"

The cousins looked at each other questioningly.

"It's not a bad idea of Jenny's," said Mrs. Swift. "It's a good school, and they take them quite young. John could easily get her nominated free. He's on the Board, and has a lot of influence. The sooner she goes, the more quickly she'd pick up English. Also she could travel with us in the car instead of your having to bring her."

Rosemary hesitated. She just didn't know what to answer. It was all so sudden. Jenny was jumping up and down in her chair in her excitement.

"Jenny gets tired of these long car drives," added Mrs. Swift. "She's always so much happier if there's another child in the car."

"I just don't know what to say," replied Rosemary. "It's most awfully kind of you . . . but somehow she seems so wee to go away just yet . . . could I think it over and give you an answer in a day or two?"

"Of course," answered Mrs. Swift. "Just let us know when you feel sure. No, Jenny, don't go on and on about it; people can't make up their minds on important matters without a little 'think' first, or they may make them up wrongly."

"I've made mine up upon this important matter,"

announced Jenny dramatically. "Oh, Auntie Rosemary, I'm sure you'll say yes. It really does seem to be the best idea I've ever had in my life. Even Mummy and Daddy thought it good!—Oh, look, Daddy, there are ice creams for pudding, the kind you don't like. Please will you pretend you'd like one, and I'll eat it for you, as well as mine."

In her excitement at the possibility of getting two ice creams Jenny forgot about Kinza for the moment, and the talk turned to other subjects. Pleasantly the evening passed, until Rosemary rose to go.

"Daddy and I will take you home," said Mrs. Swift, rising too. "Jenny, darling, run up to bed."

"All right," answered Jenny, who, having enjoyed her ice cream, was in an unusually obliging mood. She flung her arms round her aunt's neck, and drew her head down close to her mouth, so that no one could hear what they were saying.

"You are going to think hard about it, aren't you, Auntie?" she whispered.

"Yes, Jenny, very hard—I'm going to ask God to show me the right way, too."

"Do you think He'll have shown you by tomorrow morning?"

"I don't know, Jenny—it's such a big thing. Give me two days!"

"Well, ask Him to show you as quick as possible— and ask Him to let it be Yes."

"Couldn't you ask too?"

"I don't really know how to. . . . but I'll try . . . Good night, Auntie Rosemary."

"Good night, Jenny."

She loosened the child's clinging arms gently, and set out across the dark market place with Mr. and Mrs. Swift. Under the street lamp she turned to wave, and Jenny waved back. Black against the bright background of the huge doorway, a slender fairy figure standing poised on the threshold of light.

CHAPTER SIXTEEN

Kinza Disappears

HAMID WELCOMED the coming of spring for, however hardy you are, you never quite get used to blue toes and fingers and wet clinging rags, to bitter winds and driving rain and snow on bare chapped skin. But all that was over now; the sun shone warm and comforting, the storks nested in the tower, flowers clothed the mountain, and cherry and

peach blossom made the valley beautiful. Baby goats
skipped and jostled in the streets, and Hamid, like
all other young, growing things, had shot up several
inches and looked more like a little scarecrow than
ever. The clothes that the English nurse had given
him had fallen to pieces, but his rags no longer
caused him any anxiety. For six months at least the
sunshine would wrap him about and the winds
would only caress him. He stretched himself luxuri-
ously on the step of the doughnut stall, licked the oil
off his fingers, and watched the seething market
with bright observant eyes.

There was always so much to see in the square on
market days. The country women were streaming in,
strong, tanned and loud-voiced, bowed almost double
under huge loads of charcoal. Some wore straw hats
with enormous brims, and some wore strips of leather
bound round their legs. Some were quite old, panting feebly under the weight; others were still very
young and seemed almost exhausted. Then a truck
arrived, laden with boxes of silvery fish fresh from the
Mediterranean. The market loafers all surged forward
to earn a few coins by carrying the dripping boxes on
their heads to the fish market. Grubby little boys
darted in and out of the crowd trying to sell dusty
dough-rings on strings, and donkeys jostled and
brayed. Hamid chuckled as a beggar got mixed up
with a mule's back legs; then he lifted up his eyes
to the hills where snow still lingered among the high

rocks and pines. Dazzling white against dazzling blue sparkled the snow, so dazzling he could not look at it for long. He looked back at the market, seeing nothing for the brightness until his eyes focused on a patch of scarlet, and there was Kinza in a scarlet jersey prancing along between Jenny and the English nurse who had come out to do her shopping.

Then in a flash he caught sight of something else. He thought he was dreaming for a second, and rubbed the light from his eyes and looked again. He was not dreaming. He went very white under his tan, turned a backward somersault into the shop and hid himself securely between the stone oven and the counter on which the doughnuts had sizzled earlier that morning. Then he peeped out, like a startled rabbit from its hole, to watch what would happen next.

His stepfather stood rigid in a doorway opposite, staring fixedly at the little party who were unconsciously buying oranges. Then drawing a step or two nearer he watched Kinza as a snake might watch a baby rabbit at play, waiting its moment to strike. His keen eyes were taking in everything: the blind gestures, the happy freedom of her baby prattle, the stout little shoes and good warm clothes. As the three went over to the oil-merchant's he followed, coming very close to his stepdaughter, so close that for one breathless moment Hamid wondered if he was going to snatch her up. But he did not touch her. He merely moved behind them, inconspicuous in the jostling crowd, and Hamid noticed that his black eyes burned with anger and his mouth was closed as tightly as a cruel, steel trap.

Hamid, recovering from his first shock, was not afraid. His father had come over to the market on business, and would doubtless leave the town that evening. He had not seen Hamid, nor would he see him, for at the earliest possible moment Hamid would run off to the mountains, and keep company with the monkeys until after dark. For Kinza he felt not the smallest anxiety. Kinza was in the safe keeping of the English nurse who loved her and would never let her go. Her home was a fortress into which his father could never penetrate. Hamid himself would remain in his burrow until his master released him, and then—over the hills and far away.

The master arrived quite soon, and was surprised and annoyed to find his assistant under the counter instead of at it. He boxed his ears, which Hamid did not mind in the least, and cut a small sum off his pay, which he minded quite a lot. However, he soon forgot in the delight of his dangerous freedom, for the market lay between him and the mountain, and somewhere, swallowed up in the crowds, lurked his stepfather.

Darting hither and thither on nimble brown feet, he crossed the danger zone and made for the cobbled path that ran along the outskirts of the town overlooking the steep river valley below. The stream cascaded beneath him, and beyond rose the wide mountain slope, gracious and green, clouded with silver olives and foaming fruit blossom. There was one specially beautiful tree standing in the middle of a field all by itself—a double cherry in full flower, its branches bowed with the weight of its blossom. White as the river spray, white as the snow lingering on the summits, white as the page of the English nurse's little book that spoke of a heart forgiven and washed pure and clean. "Blessed are the pure in heart: for they shall see God," was the verse they always recited when the nurse held up the white page in front of them. Hamid said it to himself now as he skipped up the steep steps towards the rocks, and munched the half-loaf he had bought himself for breakfast—hot and fragrant was the bread, clean and sparkling the sunlight, and all the bright world lay in front of him. White in his heart, gladder than the sunlight, was that dawning love that he could not put into words, but which had been born in him the night he first knelt beside the charcoal pot and recited the only prayer he knew. He knew that his prayer had been answered and that since that night he had never been alone or desolate or really afraid. It was knowing this that was the deep source of his happiness, making his body feel lighter and stronger, touching the very springtime with a new radiance, greatly adding to his enjoyment of his hot loaf. Truly

blessed was Hamid that morning, as, warm with
climbing, he passed through the gate in the wall to
where a spring gushed from a pipe in the bank. He
stuck his head into the shower to cool himself, and
sat down among the periwinkles to dry.

Kinza, Jenny, and Aunt Rosemary made their way
home, and never noticed the sinister figure of the
man who followed them as far as the entrance of the
street and stood watching until the door of the house
closed behind them. It was almost time for the dispensary to open. Usually, while Aunt Rosemary
worked there, Kinza sat on the front step in the sunshine and talked to the kitten, and the patients
stepped over or round her; but during the past fortnight she had often been to play with Jenny, who
loved looking after her. So now, with her new story-
book which she had brought to show her aunt in one
hand, and Kinza holding on to the other, Jenny set off
to find her mother and father at the hotel.

The two little girls threaded their way through the
market crowds and entered the tower gardens which
lay between them and the hotel. There was no one
in the gardens, for everyone was busy buying and
selling, and the sleepy silence made her want to
linger. She thought of her new book; she had reached
such an exciting part, and this would be a lovely
quiet place to sit and read just for five minutes. Her
mother had told her she was never to loiter or sit
down betweeen her aunt's house and the hotel, but,

after all, her mother did not know what time she set out. There was a fascinating little stone nook under a wistaria curtain near the old archway that led into another part of the garden. She sat down with Kinza beside her and buried herself in the story.

It was a story after Jenny's own heart—about a child who had a pony of her own and rode just as Jenny was going to do when she got home. She hardly noticed that Kinza had risen to her feet and started to wander along the path toward the archway. Kinza often went for little walks, her arms held out in front of her to avert danger; when she felt she had gone far enough she would stand still and squeak till someone fetched her back.

Jenny read eagerly on, for she must reach the end of the chapter and discover whether Annabel's pony was going to win the cup for jumping or not. Out of the corner of her eye she could see Kinza standing in the archway. She must fetch her back in a minute, but she would be quite all right while Jenny just finished the page—and then just one page more.

She skimmed to the end and got up quickly with a sigh of relief, because Annabel had won easily. But she felt guilty at having let Kinza stray through the archway alone. "Kinza!" she called eagerly, running into the shadows and out into the sunshine of the other part of the garden, and then she stopped short and her eyes grew big with fright. For the green plot in front of her was empty and deserted—there was no sign of Kinza anywhere.

With her heart beating wildly she ran from bush to bush, searching behind every one; up and down the steps she flew, back into the walled garden, but it was no good; not a trace remained to tell which path the stumbling little feet had followed. Kinza had completely disappeared.

Jenny rushed out into the market, half-blind with panic, bumping into people and nearly treading on the goods set out for sale. People turned to look at her anxiously, pushing her way wildly in and out, with her pale, tear-stained cheeks and big, frightened eyes. They thought she had lost her mother, and pointed toward the hotel, but she only shook her head and rushed on, searching frantically.

At last she stood still, completely out of breath, and, because there was nowhere else to look, and because she did not like the people staring at her, she went back to the garden and stood alone by the fatal archway, trying to decide what to do next.

She simply could not go back to her aunt. Aunt Rosemary had trusted her alone with Kinza, and she had failed completely in her trust. What would her aunt say? and, worse still, where was Kinza? Had something terrible happened to her? Was she frightened or hurt and crying out, wondering why Jenny did not come to her? Jenny did not know. She burst into tears and ran sobbing to the hotel, up the stairs to her mother's room, and into her mother's arms.

It took Mrs. Swift some minutes to piece the confused story together, but when she finally succeeded in unraveling what had happened she went rather white, too. She dried Jenny's eyes, and took her by the hand.

"We must go and tell Auntie Rosemary at once," she said quietly. "We'll have one more look in the market place on the way."

Jenny stood quite still. "I *can't* go to Aunt Rosemary," she said tragically; "I just *can't*, Mummy. You'll have to go and tell her."

"No," said Mrs. Swift, still quietly, but very firmly, "you must come and tell her yourself. You see, Jenny, this has happened because you were disobedient and untrustworthy, and you must just be brave and take the blame you deserve. And we must go at once, because if anyone has taken Kinza every moment may matter. Daddy is on the terrace and he'll come with us."

It was a silent little party that set out from the hotel. Mr. Swift suggested that he should do one more quick search in the market place while Jenny and her mother scoured the gardens again; and they separated at the steps. Ten minutes later they met again, grave and anxious.

"Well," said Mr. Swift, "the sooner we get Rosemary on to this the better. She can speak the language and question the people."

They met Rosemary coming across the market to look for Kinza at the hotel, as it was her dinner time. Mr. Swift told her what had happened, and while he spoke Jenny stood a little apart, her eyes fixed on the ground, not daring to look at her aunt's face. She wondered what her aunt would say, and whether she would reproach her bitterly right there in the middle of the market. But, as it happened, nothing was said about her carelessness just then. Everyone seemed to have forgotten about it. All they were thinking about was Kinza.

They went back to the walled garden, to see the exact place so that Aunt Rosemary could question the shopkeepers nearest the spot, but no one could give her any news. Whatever had happened had happened just the other side of the archway, and the archway was hidden from the road by a high wall. There were three exits from that part of the garden, and one led straight out on to a lonely country road that branched off in the next couple of miles into a dozen wild mountain tracks.

"There are two possibilities," said Aunt Rosemary at last, when all questioning had proved fruitless. "One is that she has been kidnapped for the sake of her clothes, and in that case the police might help us; the other is that her own people have decided they want her back again and have stolen her away. In that case I'm afraid she has gone for good. After all, I have no claim to her against her own people. I don't even know where she came from in the first place; I only know she was not a local child . . ." She stopped abruptly as a new thought suggested itself to her. "I wonder where Hamid is," she went on eagerly. "I've often thought he had something to do with her—he might be able to give some clue."

But not one of the crowd of boys who had collected to see what was going on could tell of Hamid's whereabouts. He had been at his post that morning, and had last been seen making for the mountains. Everyone volunteered to go and look for him, and they scattered in all directions, for the rich Englishman would no doubt reward the finder handsomely. But no one succeeded in tracking him to earth, for he was far up the ravine between the great rocks, throwing stones at the monkeys. And so frightened was he of meeting his stepfather that he stayed there till long after sunset and missed the boys' meeting for the first time in many weeks.

The police, when they had heard the story, were courteous and sympathetic, but not very hopeful. They promised to telephone the Government outposts in the mountains to watch the main tracks and check up on travelers, but the countless little bypaths known only to the villagers ran far outside their reach. Besides, even if the child were found, what was there

to prove that she did not belong to her captors? They
could be fined for stealing the clothes, but the child
. . . the policeman shrugged his shoulders very ex-
pressively, lifted his eyebrows, cocked his head on
one side, and spread out both hands. There was no
more to be said.

Nor was there any more to be done, so they went
sorrowfully back to Aunt Rosemary's house to have
some tea, as everyone had been far too busy and upset to think about dinner. But none of them felt
hungry, and after a while Mr. and Mrs. Swift rose
to go, and Jenny, pale and wretched, followed them,
still not daring to look at her aunt, who, as a matter
of fact, had hardly given her naughtiness a thought.
She was far too taken up in wondering what had become of Kinza.

Rosemary was glad to be left alone. She carried
out the tea things, and then came back into her little
room and knelt down, meaning to pray for Kinza.
But the kitten sprang up beside her, mewing for its
little playmate, and under the cushion on which she
rested her arms was something hard and knobbly—
Kinza's wooden doll. She gazed round the room, and
there was Kinza's ball, Kinza's mat, Kinza's box of
sweets that Jenny had given her. Everywhere she
looked there were signs of the missing, loved little
presence, and Rosemary suddenly laid down her head
on her arms and her anxiety seemed to overwhelm
her. Where was Kinza? and what was happening to

her? How terrified and homesick she would be, how helpless in her bewildering darkness! "O God," she cried, "take care of her; don't let her be hurt or afraid; bring her back safely to me."

As she prayed, she heard a little sob behind her and realized she was not alone in the room. She looked up quickly, and there in the doorway stood Jenny, swollen-eyed with crying, her hands clasped pitifully in front of her.

"Jenny!" exclaimed Rosemary, surprised. "Does Mummy know you've come?"

"Yes," said Jenny with a gulp. "I said I must see you alone, so Mummy brought me back to the door, and you'd forgotten to bolt it, so I just came in, and she says please will you see me home when you've finished with me . . . and I don't suppose you want to see me at all . . . because . . . because . . . it was all my fault about Kinza, and oh, Auntie, what ever shall I do?"

The last words came out with a rush of fresh tears and Aunt Rosemary drew the trembling little girl into the room, shut the door and sat down beside her.

"You can't do anything, Jenny," she said gently, "but God loves Kinza far more than we do, and He can do everything. Let's kneel down and ask God together to shelter little Kinza and comfort her and keep her safe."

So they knelt side by side, and Aunt Rosemary committed Kinza to the arms of the Good Shepherd.

Jenny listened and wondered, more miserable than she had ever been before. It was all very well for Aunt Rosemary, she thought to herself. When dreadful things happened to Aunt Rosemary she had a place of refuge—a place where in any time of need she could find forgiveness and peace and comfort. But Jenny knew no such refuge. She felt shut out and in the dark. She would never forgive herself, and neither would anyone else, if Kinza were really lost.

For the first time in her life her naughtiness had really mattered, and there seemed no escape from the terrible results of it. Nearly every day she was self-willed and would have her own way and lost her temper if crossed, but Mummy and Daddy were always nice and understanding about it, and remembered that after all she had been ill for three months. Now she had gone her own way and disobeyed once too often.

"If only Kinza could come back," said Jenny to herself, "I would never be disobedient or naughty again. I'd be good for ever and ever."

CHAPTER SEVENTEEN

Hamid's Secret Revealed

ROSEMARY spent most of next day trying to trace Hamid, but Hamid was apparently determined not to be traced. On hearing early in the morning that he was urgently wanted by the English nurse, he cut work and made straight for the mountains. Why should the English nurse want him urgently just then? Perhaps his father had spoken to her and she was going to hand him over. It was all most suspicious and Hamid decided to keep clear of her.

However, the English nurse was so very much in earnest that on being told that Hamid had gone up into the mountains early she cancelled her boys' meeting and settled herself just before sunset behind the pillar of the great stone archway through which he was likely to return. She did not have to wait very long. Before the light had faded over the western ranges a weary little figure skulked in through the shadows and the English nurse grabbed hold of him by what remained of his shirt.

For a moment he struggled violently, but she spoke to him at once, and her words arrested him, so that he stood still. "Hamid," she was saying pleadingly, "I've lost Kinza. Please can you help me to find her again? Do you know where she might have gone?"

She kept tight hold of him and he stood rigidly in front of her, gazing up at her uncertainly. At first he was too startled to collect his thoughts, but gradually his mind cleared, and he began to put two and two together. If Kinza had disappeared, her father had certainly taken her home, and if the nurse was searching for her, then she certainly did not know about their father. But it did not seem safe to tell: it might lead to contact with the police, and no little outlaw boy ever wishes to have anything to do with the police; or it might lead to meeting his people—

or it might all be a trick or a trap. It was far safer to deny all knowledge and have nothing to do with it.

And yet if he refused to speak, Kinza was lost, and all his efforts were wasted; and Kinza had been so happy, so fat, so safe. Now she would be sold to the beggar—why else should his father want her?—and he would not be there to protect her.

"I don't know anything about it," he said warily, after a long pause, but his eyes, by the light of the archway lamp, were bright and starry with unshed tears at the thought of Kinza; and the nurse, seeing them and noting the pause, felt quite sure that he knew a great deal about it—though it might be very difficult to worm it out of him. She must proceed with the utmost tact and care.

"Let's go home and have some supper together," she said soothingly, "and we can talk about it in the house. You must be hungry after being on the mountain all day."

He had shared a piece of rye bread with a shepherd boy at midday, but apart from that he had had nothing to eat since the evening before, having forfeited his work and his wages, and he was ravenously, wolfishly hungry. There was a gnawing pain inside him, and unless he accepted the English nurse's offer there was very little hope of food that night. It was rather rash to go to her house, because after all it might be a trick, but nobody could make him talk. His hunger overcame his caution. He slipped a dirty little hand into the hand of the English nurse, and she clasped it firmly and let go the scruff of his neck. She did not let go his hand until they were safely inside the house with the door locked behind them.

She led Hamid upstairs to the room where he had once seen Kinza asleep, and he sat down cross-legged on the mat, tense with excitement, and sniffed rapturously, for the pot was on the fire, and the house was full of the fragrant odor of hot rice and vegetables cooked in olive oil. She brought him a steaming bowlful and a great hunk of bread, and then fetched her own and sat down on the mattress near him. She did not question him while he ate, for he was completely absorbed in his food, but she watched him thoughtfully. He was so like Kinza in looks—the same dark bright eyes set widely apart under a broad forehead; the same heart-shaped face, the broad cheek bones tapering to a beautifully molded little chin, and the same determined mouth. She waited until the last delicious drop of food had gone, and the bowl wiped clean with a crust of bread, and then she spoke with a certainty that she did not feel.

"Hamid," she said very firmly, "do you know who has stolen away your little sister Kinza? If you know, you must tell me, because I want to get her back."

The English nurse was very tired, very strained, very afraid that her guess was wrong. Her voice, which had been so firm, quivered a little as she finished speaking, and that quiver reassured Hamid.

This was no trick, no scheme to catch him out. It was the honest cry of a loving heart, and Hamid wriggled closer, and squatted with his head close to her knees, his flushed face upturned to hers. "I think my stepfather has got her," he replied. "I saw him watching her in the market yesterday. He followed her right across the Square, but I thought she was safe with you."

If the nurse was startled by her success she did not show it. Any false move might scare him into silence. She went on speaking very quietly.

"Where does your stepfather live?"

Hamid told her the name of the village.

"Did he not know she was with me?"

"No."

The English nurse made another guess.

"Why did you put her in my hall that night?"

"My mother told me to."

"Why?"

"My father did not want Kinza. He was going to sell her to a beggar. Kinza would have been very unhappy, so my mother sent her to you."

"And now?"

"My father will sell her to the beggar. He wants the money."

The nurse shuddered. Kinza's prospects were far worse than she had even imagined, and she must save her somehow. She went on quietly questioning:

"How far is the village?"

"Two days' journey on a horse—but my father probably came by road on a market truck. That only takes
about six hours."

"And you—how did you come?"

"Partly on a truck—mostly walking."

"And Kinza?"

"On my back."

He spoke in the tones he would have used had he
been speaking of a walk up the street, and the nurse
marveled at his courage; surely he, who had dared
so much for Kinza's sake, would help her now!

"And if I went to your village, and offered to pay
your father more than the beggar, would he let me
buy back Kinza?"

"I don't know; he might. But how would you know
the house? There are many parts of the village with
hills between."

"You must come with me and show me."

"I can't. My father would beat me dreadfully if I
went home."

"You need not come home. You can point out the
house from a distance."

"But everyone in the village knows me. They will
tell my father."

"We will arrive after sunset in the car of the Englishman. No one will see you in the dark. Surely you
will do this to save Kinza!"

She had leaned forward in her earnestness and laid
her hands on his shoulders, and he sat there scratch-

ing his head doubtfully, battling with his fears.

"Hamid," she pleaded, "if you refuse I shan't be able to find her. The beggar will have her, and she will suffer and be cold and hungry in the streets of a big city, and all her life she'll live in the dark. If she comes back to me she will be happy, and I will teach her about the Lord Jesus, and she'll grow up with her heart full of light and happiness—I've told you about Him so many times, Hamid. Do you believe in Him yet?"

He glanced up at her, his face bright with shy love.

"I love the Lord Jesus very much," he replied simply. "He has taken my sins away, and He has made my heart happy."

The nurse caught at his words eagerly.

"Then He can also take your fears away and make your heart brave," she urged. "It says in God's Book that the perfect love of Jesus in our hearts casts out our fear. There isn't any more room for it. Let's ask Him now, Hamid, to cast out your fear and to save Kinza."

He shut his eyes obediently, held out his cupped hands as though to receive some poured-out blessing, and as the nurse prayed he repeated the words after her, and made them his own. While he was speaking two thoughts came into his mind: if the Lord Jesus really loved him. He would not let his father beat him, and therefore there was nothing to be afraid of; and what fun it would be to drive all the way to his village in the Englishman's big, fast, grey car.

So even while he prayed, the Spirit of God breathed happy, brave thoughts into his troubled heart, so when they had finished praying he was quite ready to agree to the nurse's suggestions, and finally left the house in a state of pleasant excitement. As he wandered across the market place he saw himself sitting upright at the car window, waving proudly, and his friends, green with envy, watching his royal progress spellbound. He suddenly chuckled with glee and skipped in the air. The warm night breezes fanned his hot cheeks, and he thrilled to the adventure. About the final result he had no doubt at all. His father would do anything for money, and the nurse would certainly offer more than the beggar would give.

As soon as he had left the house, Rosemary set off for the hotel to lay her plan before Mr. and Mrs. Swift. She had not seen them since early morning, when they had been round to say that Jenny seemed so restless and upset that they had decided to go for a long motor drive into the mountains and take a picnic dinner. Jenny, full of impossible plans for rescuing Kinza, had not wished to go at all, but her father had insisted. There had been a scene in consequence, and they had driven off with Jenny looking like a sulky thundercloud, hunched up in the back of the car.

She found them sitting in the lounge looking tired and depressed. They had been to her house earlier to inquire if there was any news, but she had been up at the Gate watching for Hamid. They jumped up at the sight of her.

"Has anything happened?" they asked eagerly.

"Yes," said Rosemary, unable to hide her excitement. She dropped into an empty chair, and leaning forward she poured out the wonderful story.

"Of course, I've gone and fixed it all up with Hamid without consulting you," she ended; "but I felt quite, quite sure you'd be willing, because you've been so sweet about Kinza. We would have to start tomorrow afternoon—it's about four hours' drive—in order to arrive soon after sunset. Then Hamid says it's a good walk on beyond where the car can go. We should not be back till the small hours of the morning, but I didn't think you'd mind that for once."

"Of course not," Mrs. Swift assured her, as eager as she was. "John shall take you and Hamid, and I'll stay with Jenny. I don't think she ought to go. I know she could sleep in the car, but it means rousing her in the middle of the night when we get home."

"There'll be no end of a rumpus if she's left behind," said her father, and the eagerness vanished from their faces and they both sighed.

"Is Jenny in bed?" inquired Rosemary. "Could I tell her all about it, or will she be asleep?"

Mr. and Mrs. Swift glanced at each other, and

there was a moment's silence. Then Mrs. Swift spoke.

"Yes, do go and tell her," she said, "and, Rosemary, I wish you could somehow talk her into a better frame of mind. She's so fond of you, and I don't seem able to do anything with her tonight. We've had such a miserable day. She sulked and grumbled from the moment we set out till the moment we got home—because she didn't want to come at all. She wanted to stay and help you look for Kinza. Of course, I know she's been ill and all that, but really she does behave like a spoiled baby when she can't get her own way."

"So I sent her to bed when we got in," added Mr. Swift gloomily. "Her tempers are getting too much of a good thing. She's not used to being punished and took it very badly, so I don't know what sort of a mood you'll find her in, poor little girl. She'll certainly kick up an awful fuss if she's not allowed to go tomorrow."

"Poor Jenny!" said Aunt Rosemary. "I'll go and see if she's still awake," and she climbed the stairs rather slowly and knocked at the door. There was no answer. She opened the door and went in.

"What do you want?" said a sullen voice from under the bedclothes. "I haven't gone to sleep early like you said, so you needn't think I have!"

"It's me, Jenny," said Aunt Rosemary quietly, and went over and sat down on the bed.

Jenny came out at once, rather embarrassed, for she always spoke politely in front of Aunt Rosemary, wishing to keep up the picture of herself as a pleasant child. However, Mummy and Daddy had probably been telling about her, and she must make Auntie Rosemary see her point of view. Mummy and Daddy completely misunderstood her and were cross with her when they should have been sorry for her, but surely her aunt would understand and be nice and see how ill-used she was.

"Oh, Auntie Rosemary," cried Jenny bursting into tears; "I'm so glad you've come! I've been thinking about Kinza all day long."

"Oh, no, you haven't," replied Aunt Rosemary in a very matter-of-fact voice. "You've been thinking about yourself all day long, and that's why you are so unhappy. Selfish people are always unhappy because they mind so much when they can't have their own way."

"I'm *not* selfish," sobbed Jenny angrily. "You don't understand any more than Mummy and Daddy do. I couldn't stop wondering where Kinza was, and they took me right away where I couldn't find out or hear if there was any news."

"But your hearing the news wouldn't have helped Kinza at all," replied Aunt Rosemary. "It would just have satisfied your curiosity. And because you couldn't be satisfied you made Mummy and Daddy

miserable all day. And if that's not selfish I don't
know what is."

Jenny could think of nothing to say to that, so she
merely repeated forlornly, "You don't understand."

"Oh, Jenny, Jenny, I understand so well," cried
Aunt Rosemary, suddenly kneeling down and drawing the angry, hot little girl toward her. "I understand that because you have always had everything
you want, and because Mummy and Daddy have always given you such lovely things, and been so good to
you, you think nothing matters in the world except
your own happiness. Your heart is like a little closed-
in circle with yourself in the middle, and every time
anything happens that hurts or annoys you, you think
the world is coming to an end. And as you get older,
Jenny, you will find that there are more and more
things that will annoy and hurt you, and you are going to grow up into such a very unhappy, unloving
woman. You see, you haven't really time or room to
love anyone else properly because all your love is
being poured in on yourself."

Jenny was quite silent. No one had ever talked to
her like this before. Her mother and father usually
ended these affairs by saying, "Never mind, darling;
we're sure you didn't mean it. Let's forget all about
it."

But perhaps Auntie Rosemary was partly speaking
the truth. It was worrying to remember how often
she felt very, very unhappy, simply because it was

not always possible for her to have her own way.
How lovely it would be to be the sort of person who
was always happy and who did not seem to mind
very much if she couldn't have what she wanted!
There was a girl at school, for instance, who had
wanted to learn riding, and who had wanted a new
dress for the party, but she couldn't have either because her father couldn't afford it. Yet she had kept
quite calm about it and had seemed to enjoy the party
in a dress of her sister's. Jenny could not understand
it, and decided she was simply made differently.

"I can't help minding things," said Jenny at last,
in a small grieved voice. "And I do love people. I
love Mummy and Daddy and you and Kinza and
lots of people."

"Only as long as we please you," replied Aunt Rosemary. "Directly we stop doing what you want you
are quite happy to make us miserable, as you've made
Mummy and Daddy miserable today."

Jenny was silent again, but she had drawn very
close to the kneeling figure beside her. It was no good
trying to go on making Auntie Rosemary admire her,
because apparently she knew all about her, and in
that knowledge there was a curious kind of peace.
Jenny suddenly felt she could drop all pretences and
utter what is the real deep but sometimes unrecog-
nized longing of every child's heart.

"I *do* want to be good and happy," she whispered,
"and I *do* want to make Mummy happy. But I can't.

I just seem to mind things so much that I can't help being cross."

"Yes," agreed Aunt Rosemary thoughtfully, "I know. Our own selves with all their wantings and mindings are very, very difficult to move out of the center of the circle. In fact, I know only one way to do it. That is to ask the Lord Jesus to come into the circle with His wishes and to turn out self. At first it's not easy because your self keeps wanting things as well, and you have to keep saying, 'Not my will, but Yours.' But after a time a wonderful thing happens. As we learn to know the Lord Jesus, and talk to Him, and as He talks to us, we gradually come to love Him so much that His wishes become our wishes, and we begin to want only the things He wants. It says in the Bible that when we want the same thing as the Lord Jesus, we only have to ask for it and we get it. Then of course we are perfectly satisfied, happy people."

"I don't see how you mean," whispered Jenny sorrowfully.

"No," agreed Aunt Rosemary. "It does sound rather difficult, doesn't it? But it is really quite simple if you think of it like this. It all starts by asking the Lord Jesus to forgive us and to turn out our selfishness, and to come in and live in the center of our lives instead. When He comes we shall start loving Him, because He loves us so much. When you love people you want to look at them and get near to them.

When you look at Jesus and come near to Him, you grow like Him, and you want what He wants. It's like looking at something very bright, and reflecting the light so that you look bright yourself."

"Oh, I see," said Jenny, rather sleepily. She had stopped crying and was lying very still. Aunt Rosemary waited a moment and then said, "I really came to tell you some news of Kinza. We've discovered where she's gone, and tomorrow your father and Hamid and I are going to her home, and we are going to try to persuade her father to let us have her back."

"Oh, where? when? how?" cried Jenny, springing up in bed. "Tell me all about it quick! Can I come, too?"

"No," said Aunt Rosemary, "you can't. Mummy says it's too late, and probably in a native village the fewer of us the better. You've got a good chance to make up for today by obeying without any sulking or crossness. Now I'll tell you how I found out, and all about it," and as she told it, Jenny lay and listened in an unusually humble frame of mind.

It was all going to come right after all, perhaps, and she did not deserve it. Last night she had made a sort of promise—"If Kinza comes back I'm going to be good for ever and ever."

"Auntie," she whispered penitently, her face half-buried in the pillow, "tell Mummy to come. I want to tell her I'm sorry, and I want to tell her I'll be good tomorrow."

CHAPTER EIGHTEEN

A Daring Plan

THE NEXT DAY dawned bright and clear, and the rescue party set off early in the afternoon. Jenny, desperately disappointed that she was not going too, but determined to make the best of it, stood in the middle of the sunlit market place and waved them off, her hand clasped in her mother's. Hamid, all his fears forgotten in the thrill of being inside the beau-

200

tiful car, sat like some small royal personage in the back seat and nodded condescendingly to the crowd of open-mouthed, admiring urchins running behind. Far down the road they followed, shouting and hooting, rags fluttering, until the car gathered speed and raced away from them. Hamid stuck his cropped head far out of the window and yelled with triumph, and Rosemary pulled him in again by the seat of his trousers.

It was a beautiful drive. Hamid remembered the hot dusty evening when he had toiled up the same white hill, with Kinza on his back. He had been too tired then to look about him and admire the view, but now he was anxious to see all there was to see, and he leaped from side to side of the car like a tame monkey in a cage. Everywhere he looked he could see sloping fields of young wheat, tender green in the sunlight, or bright banks of flowers. Little streams rushed under the road and foamed downhill to meet the river—a blue strip in the valley below them winding between the oleanders. Little black lambs and baby goats leaped in the pastures on wobbly legs, and here and there they would see men ploughing with rough wooden ploughs and pairs of fawn oxen, yoked on top of their heads. These men were ploughing in hope, for the rainy season was almost over. Soon the drought and heat would dry up the rivers and the stream, and the countryside, now green as a garden, would become scorcl   and yellow.

They reached the level river-road in the valley, and the car sped along between low hillocks starred with bushes of white flowers. The golden air was heavy with their fragrance, and Hamid, suddenly tired by his exertions, curled up on the seat and fell fast asleep. He slept for some time, and when he woke the car had stopped on the crest of a hill. Wherever you looked, backward, forward, to left or right, you could see mountains. The Englishman and the nurse were drinking tea out of a thermos bottle, and eating sandwiches. Hamid stuck his head over the back of the seat to show he was awake, and was given a big round bun with sugar on top; and as he settled himself among the leather cushions, and licked the sugar off first, he wondered whether Heaven could hold any improvements.

Only one thought dimmed his pleasure. As the sun sank toward the western mountains, bathing the world in its long unearthly rays, the grey car was traveling toward his village and his father. The big Englishman and the nurse had promised that he should be kept safe, so he was not really very afraid. Only it was a sobering thought, and he laid his head on his arms on the window ledge and pondered it in silence. He was drawing near to his mother, too, and his heart cried out for his mother. It would be hard to be so near and yet unable to see her or speak to her. Two big tears brimmed up in his eyes and trickled over on to the shiny leather.

The nurse heard a sniff, and looked round to see a drooping little figure with tears trickling down its face. She put out her hand and laid it on his grubby knees, but he was only a little comforted. She was kind and good and the best friend he had—but she was not his mother.

Then the car swung off into a main road, leaving a town on the right. They were heading straight for the city, and big cars whizzed past them, as magnificent as their own. Hamid forgot his sorrows temporarily and began careering from side to side again, thrilled by the gleaming bonnets and flashing windscreens. If only they were going right on to the city by the sea where great ships lay at anchor in the harbor! But they were not; for after a short while they turned aside up a mountain road and traveled on between scrubby hills where the villages of the tribespeople nestled, straw-thatched, in the hollows.

Behind these hills the sun set in a glory of blinding light. Children were bringing their goats home, and several times the car had to stop while a small figure and its flock, black against the orange west, crossed the road. Then the light faded and dusk fell, warm and kind, and Hamid could see the shape of his own home mountain in the distance with two bright stars twinkling above it. His heart began to beat very fast and his mouth felt rather dry. But the car was traveling slowly because of the stony country road, jolting them in their seats.

It was quite dark when they reached the well-known market place, with its rustling eucalyptus trees and the government buildings white in the moonlight. They drove on unchallenged beyond the few native shops to where the rough road dwindled into a track, and there Mr. Swift brought the car to a standstill.

Hamid tumbled out and ran behind an olive tree while the nurse spoke to a boy standing in the doorway of a house, and asked him to mind the car. He knew this boy, and did not wish to be recognized by anyone. He was thankful for the dark wrapping him round and for the sprouting wheat on either side of the track, into which he could scuttle at a moment's notice. He waited till the boy's back was turned, and then came skulking out from his hiding-place and without a word set off uphill along the familiar path at a great pace, with Mr. Swift and the nurse hurrying along behind him. The night seemed alive with memories, and the river below, where he had so often watered his goats, gleamed tranquil in the moonlight. This was the very track up which he had toiled on hot summer evenings carrying Kinza home from market; here was the fountain where he and Rahma had filled the buckets on dewy mornings at sunrise; to his left was the burying ground, with the three little graves where the marigolds grew, and there in front of him at the top of the hill gleamed the lights in the cottages on the outskirts of the village. Just another fifty yards' climb and he could see his own lamp-lit doorway and the rosy glow of the charcoal fire. He stopped short and beckoned his followers to his side. They were very much out of breath, for he was far more nimble than they were.

"There," he breathed, pointing toward it. "It is the third house beyond the fig tree. You just push the gate open—there is no latch. Don't be afraid of the dog—he's chained—and remember you have promised not to tell my father."

"Yes, Hamid," said the nurse quietly, "I've promised, and if your father comes with us to the car you must just hide till he goes away. We will not leave without you. Otherwise we'll meet you here."

They went cautiously on up the rocky path and Hamid went off to hide himself safely behind the bushes at the bottom of the burying ground. Crouching there, hugging his knees, he remembered his first escape, when he had crept down the hill at midnight and felt so afraid of evil spirits in the dark. Suddenly he realized that he was not afraid any more, and wondered why.

He soon remembered why. There was a hymn the English nurse had taught him, beginning "There is a beautiful Country." To those like himself whose hearts had been made white, death was no more a place of shadows and lost spirits—it was simply a door into the light and sunshine of God's Home, and the nurse had said that little children who had no knowledge of good and evil were welcome there, so probably his little brothers and sister were safe and sheltered and happy after all. Hamid suddenly wished he could go there, too, instead of crouching at the portal, an outcast within sight of his home. He yearned for the warm fireside, for the nuzzling goats, for Rahma, and, above all, for his mother. His heart strained toward her, crying out speechlessly in the dark. Surely she would hear and come.

Mr. Swift and Rosemary reached the outskirts of the village, and by the light of a torch made their way single file along the mud track that led to Hamid's home. Nobody saw them passing, and when they reached the gate, it was as he had said. It opened with a gentle push, and they stepped out of the shadows and stood hesitating in the light that streamed through the open doorway.

There was the rattle of a chain and the big black dog leaped up and strained on his lead. The bearded man sitting just inside glanced out, saw them, and rose instantly and crossed the hut. There seemed to be a sort of scuffle inside, a quick murmur of low voices, and then the master of the house appeared, smiling and bowing and full of polite greetings. He begged his guests to enter and tell their business inside, and to partake of his meal even though the food was poor. Stooping they passed through the low doorway and stood in the tiny dim room, looking round.

There was a young woman with a sad, patient face

squatting by the fire and a shy little dark-eyed girl nestling against her. In a shadowed corner leaning against a bundled blanket sat an older woman. She did not come forward to greet them; she remained in her corner, silent and watchful, and the master of the house spread a sheepskin and bade his guests sit down with their backs to her.

Of Kinza there was no sign at all, and the nurse's heart sank—perhaps they had all come on a wild-goose chase.

Expressing polite surprise at the late hour of their visit, the black-bearded man told the young woman to serve them with sweet mint tea, and as they sipped he inquired of their errand.

"I have come to find out about your little blind girl, Kinza," replied the English nurse speaking very firmly. "She was left in my charge by her brother about seven months ago. I have grown very fond of the child, and would very much like to have her back. She is your child, and it must be as you wish, but I am willing to pay a price for her—and of course her mother can come and see her from time to time."

There was an instant's silence while the stepfather, completely taken by surprise by the assurance in her voice, hesitated. She had mentioned paying a price, and he would do almost anything for money; she would pay more than the beggar. On the other hand he might get into trouble for having taken her, and there was the question of her fine clothes. Kinza had arrived home after dark, wrapped in a potato sack, and had been kept out of sight ever since. He had sold her clothes to some Spaniards that very morning. It was too much to risk. He settled his face into a state of bewildered astonishment and spread out his hands, palm upward.

"But I know nothing of the child," he assured her in an injured voice. "True, her brother stole her away some seven months ago, but since then I have neither seen her nor received news of her. If the boy has told you that this is her home, he is speaking the truth, but the child is not here, nor do I know of her whereabouts. If I hear news of her, I will gladly bring her to you."

There was a long pause. Rosemary's eyes met the eyes of the young woman sitting the other side of the fire. They were fixed on her very steadily and—was it imagination, or did she really give a very faint nod in the direction of the old woman?

Rosemary turned on her sheepskin and looked all round the room. There was only one possible place of concealment, and that was under the blanket behind the old woman. No longer caring anything about manners, she got up suddenly and stepped across the room, and called out Kinza's name at the top of her voice three times over.

The man stood on his feet, pale with fright; the old woman clutched at the rug, but she was too late. Kinza, who had been suddenly lifted from her mother's arms and dumped on a cold floor, was only sleeping very lightly. At the sound of the well-known, well-loved voice she sprang up with a loud answering cry. The old woman would have held her down, but her frantic struggles under the blanket betrayed her. Rosemary almost lifted the old woman out of the way, flung back the covering, and the next moment Kinza was in her arms, clinging to her as though she would never let go.

Kinza's joy was indescribable; all the terror was over and she was safe again in the strong arms of her protector. The last two-and-a-half days had been a sort of nightmare of jolting and cold as she had lain all night wrapped in a sack on the boards of a truck; of cuffs when she cried, of hunger and fear and bewilderment, and of rough hands that snatched her from her mother's arms. But that was all over now; the voice she loved had called her to safety, and no one, she was certain, could ever pluck her out of that sure clasp. Her strained body relaxed and she lay at peace. Rosemary turned to face the stepfather.

He had risen threateningly, his face pale with anger and fear, and Mr. Swift had risen too and stood ready to interpose. Mr. Swift was a big man, and Si Mohamed realized in a moment that his only hope now was to give in graciously and strike a good bargain. His expression changed almost instantly to forced amusement at Kinza's joy.

"There," he said laughing in rather a nervous way,

"you have found her, and now she shall be your daughter. You are very welcome to her, and with you I know she will be safe and happy. Now what are you willing to pay for her? and she is yours!"

Rosemary, who had obtained all details from Hamid, mentioned a sum considerably higher than the beggar had offered. Si Mohamed, terrified that clothes were going to be mentioned and only anxious to get rid of his unwelcome guests, closed with the offer at once. He came forward to receive his price full of polite expressions of delight that Kinza should be so honored. But Kinza, hearing the dreaded voice approaching, gave a little scream and, flinging her arms tight round Rosemary's neck, clung to her terrified.

Rosemary, handing over the money, stooped over the frightened child. "It's all right, Kinza," she whispered. "Don't be afraid. He can't touch you. You're my little girl now."

And Kinza, reassured and trustful, stuck two fingers into her mouth and lay still and content. She did not know that a long journey had been taken for her sake and that a high price had been paid to buy her back again, but the voice that had never yet told her a lie had said, "Don't be afraid; you're my little girl now." So Kinza was not afraid any longer. Right there in the presence of her enemy, resting in the arms of her friend, she fell asleep.

There was nothing left to do but to get away as quickly as possible before any further trouble arose. Rosemary said a brief good by to the old woman and the stepfather and turned to speak to the mother, but her seat by the charcoal pot was empty. Only a little girl sat watching, solemn and big-eyed. The mother had slipped out unnoticed while the payment was being arranged, and, caring nothing for her husband's anger or the fact that her action would seem out of place, she was hurrying down the steep path that led from the village, stumbling in the darkness, calling softly and breathlessly to her son.

She guessed he must be near at hand, for how else could they have found the house? But even so she was startled when a little white-gowned figure, looking like an angel in the moonlight, ran out from the shadows of the olives on the outskirts of the burying grounds and kissed her hand. She drew him fearfully back into the dark retreat of the trees and, crouching against a gnarled old trunk, she scanned his upturned face yearningly. "Little son, little son," she whispered, for she knew their time was short, "is it well with you? Is there no evil to you?"

"No evil to me!" he whispered back. "I work in the town and all is well—but Kinza—and my father—have they got her?"

His mother nodded. "The English woman paid a price for her and will take her as her daughter. I have

no more fear for Kinza. All will be well for her and
she will never suffer or be beaten or beg. But you,
little son . . . come back to me. I miss you so."

He shook his head slowly. "I daren't," he breathed.
"My father would kill me with beating. I have work
and can live, and the English nurse feeds us at night.
Besides, she has a Book about Jesus, the Man she told
you about who took children in His arms, and in that
Book is written the way of God which leads to
Heaven. What she tells us from her Book makes my
heart happy and I must know more."

He was speaking very earnestly and she drew him
close against her. He had grown taller, but he was so
thin, and to her he still seemed such a little boy; yet
all on his own he had found a way of happiness. A
moonbeam had struck through the silver leaves and
she could see his face brighten as he spoke. If only
she could follow him. She had no happiness.

"Then you must come and tell me, little son," she
urged. "I want to be happy too. Your father won't
beat you. He has to pay a boy to look after his goats,
and he often grumbles because you are not here to
work for him. He would be glad to see you back."

He rested his head against her shoulder and sat
very still thinking hard. He was tired of traveling and
wandering and fending for himself, tired of trying to
be a man before his time. All he wanted was to be a
little boy again, and to lean unashamed against his
mother in the dark for a while and then to go home.

But if he did that, he would never learn to read from the nurse's Book and perhaps he would forget the way to Heaven. Besides, he was still very afraid of his father. Slowly, and after a long silence, he made up his mind.

"I will go back now," he whispered, "and I'll learn to read from the Book that tells the way to Heaven. Then when the harvest is ripe I'll come home and tell you all about it. Only ask my father not to beat me."

Steps sounded on the path and the light of a torch was flashed on to them. They rose quickly and came out into the open moonlight. The mother stooped and kissed her baby furtively, whispered a blessing on the nurse and gave her hand to her son. Then without another word she turned up the hill and went back to the punishment that awaited her, content and unafraid. Kinza was safe forever, and she had seen her little boy. All was well with him and he had promised to come home. Nothing else mattered.

The little party hurried toward the valley. Mr. Swift had taken Kinza, and Rosemary held the torch; Hamid bounded ahead knowing every inch of the way. They had almost reached the car when they heard quick steps behind them and angry shouting. It was Si Mohamed, coming after his runaway boy. His wife's disappearance had roused his suspicions. The quiet joy in her face on her return had confirmed them.

"My father!" gasped Hamid and he made for the

car like a hunted rabbit. Finding the door locked, he
stood jumping up and down, squeaking with fear.
The nurse, still nimble in spite of her grey hair, was
only a few seconds behind him, and the big Englishman tossed Kinza into her arms as though she was a
bundle of washing, jammed the key into the lock,
dived into the front, trod on the starter, and opened
the back. The nurse, Kinza, and Hamid all seemed to
fall in at once as the car moved off with a triumphant
roar. It shot past the empty market place at thirty
miles an hour, bumping horribly, leaving Si Mohamed
standing alone with his shadow under the eucalyptus
trees, very angry and out of breath, while his grace-
less stepson flung himself back against the shiny
cushions and broke into a peal of laughter.

Five minutes later they had all settled themselves
comfortably and got over their fright. Kinza slept
deeply and peacefully, worn out by the terror and un-
certainty of the past three days. Hamid rested his
brown arms on the window, and his gaze wandered to
the twin peaks above his home, high and aloof, dwelling among the lights of God. In their bosom nestled
his own village where the name of Jesus as Saviour
had never yet been breathed, but he no longer felt
homesick or desolate. For he knew that he would
come back, alone and on foot, one summer evening
when the fields were ripe to harvest. And he would
not feel very afraid, for certainly there would be a
light on the homeward path even brighter than sun-

shine or the corn, dispelling the darkness of sin and fear. Jesus had said, "I am the light of the world: he that followeth me shall not walk in darkness, but shall have the light of life."

CHAPTER NINETEEN

A Lovely Day for a Picnic

As HAMID SPED down the road in the car, Jenny stood
waving him off in the market, swallowing down
her bitter disappointment and twisting her face into
a smile. She was determined to be good about it, and
to give her mother a happy day, but she was finding
it very difficult, because to drive to Hamid's village
in the mountains and help carry off Kinza from a

wicked stepfather would have been the greatest adventure she could possibly imagine—it sounded exactly like the best kind of fairy story. Yet here she was, standing in the market place, left behind, while the car sped away without her, and to make it even duller she had promised to be good. If she could have got into a real rage and kicked somebody she felt it might somehow have been easier to bear, though she knew that would only have made things worse, in the end.

So she kept her promise valiantly, turned a resolute face to her mother, and inquired meekly what she would like to do next.

Her mother, realizing how very valiant her little daughter was being, was only too eager to meet her half-way and give her as pleasant a time as possible. It was a lovely day, and the hills, beautiful with blossom, rose invitingly behind them.

"It's just right for a picnic!" said Mrs. Swift gaily, "and we haven't finished the book about Annabel yet. Let's go round the market and buy something nice for tea, and then we'll go across the valley and sit in the sun. You haven't found any more wild flowers lately either for that collection you were going to take back to school, and we shall be leaving in a few days now."

Jenny brightened up slightly. She could not really feel interested in Annabel or wild flowers or anything else until she knew whether Kinza was safe or not, but

a picnic with her mother would be fun, and it would
perhaps make the time pass a little more quickly.
Jenny felt she could not live through the long hours
that must elapse before they came back unless she
had something very definite to do. So she ran indoors
willingly enough, and they wandered round the market and bought bananas and nutty biscuits and a hot
loaf. The shopkeeper was asleep in the sun, but they
woke him up by prodding him.

The hotel people filled their thermos bottle, and
they cut honey sandwiches in their bedroom. Then
they set off with a basket containing tea, the story-
book, Mrs. Swift's sketching-block, and Jenny's
flower-press. Jenny, who was naturally rather lazy,
actually offered to carry it. Her mother glanced at
her a little anxiously and wondered if she was going
to be ill, but she looked quite healthy and rosy, if
rather more sober and silent than usual. So they left
the town hand in hand, walking down the steep cobbled street which led out through the crumbling wall
into the valley. Framed in the old arched gate rose
the steep olive-groves across the river bathed in sunshine, and the cherry tree standing by itself in the
middle of a field of young wheat was still bowed with
blossom. Out they passed into the light and freedom
of the open country, and crossed a humpy stone
bridge with ivy trailing over its walls. Then they
started to climb through orchards and groves until
they reached the uncultivated hillside where mari-

golds, daisies and buttercups made gardens among the rocks. Here they settled themselves. Jenny lay flat on her back and stared up at the blue sky, and her mother read two chapters of the Annabel story aloud. Then, noticing that the child was far away in thought, and not really listening, she put the book down and suggested tea.

Tea was fun. Looking across to the white town clinging to the steep hillside, they picked out their bedroom windows in the hotel, and Auntie Rosemary's roof, and the stork's nest on top of the fort, and Jenny, who had been unable to eat much dinner on account of the lump of disappointment in her throat, discovered she was hungry. Her mother was delighted, and plied her with honey sandwiches and bananas until there was not a crumb left. After this Mrs. Swift began to sketch the city gate and the ivy bridge and Jenny wandered off by herself to look for wild flowers.

She wanted to be by herself, because she wanted to think; even her mother, dear and understanding as she was, could not enter into these new thoughts that had come to her during the last few days. She could not explain to anyone how desperately she minded about Kinza; if only Kinza came back she felt the past could be forgiven and forgotten and she could somehow start life all over again. She was so tired of the old life of losing her temper and being miserable and making her mother miserable, and spoiling things that should have been happy whether she wanted to or not. Up to a few days ago she had thought there was no help for it, but Auntie Rosemary had told her there was a way of escape and, dimly understanding, Jenny believed her.

She forgot all about the wild flowers and sat down on a rock, her chin resting on her hands, trying to remember. At first she could not get it straight at all, and then she noticed a patch of buttercups growing at her feet, their faces upturned to the westering sun, golden bright. "It's like looking at something very bright and reflecting the light," was the way Aunt Rosemary had put it, and certainly each wide-open buttercup, its petal curled back in an abandonment of receiving, seemed to be reflecting the whole circle. But there were buds too, with the petals tight closed on their dark hearts. Perhaps tomorrow they would open, and Jenny wondered what it felt like when the first petal drew back and the first beam stole in. Perhaps they opened at dawn when the light was cool and silver, or in the evening when the light was golden and mellow. Jenny did not know, but because God's Holy Spirit was seeking her and teaching her she did know that hearts closed to the Lord Jesus were like flower-buds closed to the sun.

If only she knew more about the Lord Jesus, or if only she had a Bible and could read about Him! She thought rather vaguely of the picture in the dispensary, and it reassured her. He was a Person so loving

that children were not afraid of Him, and He wanted
to come into her dark, closed heart, flooding it with
light—comforting, forgiving, healing. And little by
little, perhaps quite quickly, her cross, spoiled, vain
little self would give way to the radiant Guest, and
the strong, joyful, loving Presence within her would
shine out making her strong and joyful and loving too.
"Like putting a candle inside an empty lantern so the
beams shine out," Aunt Rosemary had said. She had
specially remembered that bit.

"Please come, please come," she whispered, and
lifted her face expectantly to the sun, one in spirit
with the wide-open buttercups. Then she heard her
mother's voice calling her, and got up and ran into
her arms, her eyes starry bright with her new dis-
covery.

"Darling Mummy!" she cried, hugging her, and
then, suddenly shy, she went leaping off down the
hill laughing and skipping over the rocks and waving
her arms in the air as though carried away by some
secret joy. And her mother coming behind with the
basket wondered what had happened, but was too
wise to ask. She knew that children's most precious
thoughts can never be told to anyone. They are like
music that cannot be clothed in words and so fragile
that they would break in the telling.

She caught up on Jenny at the ivy bridge some ten
minutes later. Jenny was playing Pooh-sticks—throwing a stick into the pool above the bridge and then

rushing madly across to watch it come out the other side. She had some sticks ready for her mother, and they each threw one in together and pretended they were the Oxford and Cambridge boat race. It was quite a good game and they played it for some time. When at length they climbed the cobbled steps to the hotel the sun was setting, and the sky, framed in the city gate, was the color of ripe apricots. The day that Jenny had thought was going to last forever had come to an end quite quickly, and an hour later she was sitting up in bed and her mother was brushing her hair.

"Mummy," said Jenny.

"Yes, darling."

"I'm quite certain I shan't go to sleep till they come, but, just supposing by accident I did go to sleep, will you promise to wake me?"

Mrs. Swift hesitated. To wake Jenny was the last thing she wished to do, but then Jenny had been so sweet and good all day and to refuse might put her in a bad temper and spoil it all. "Very well, darling," she agreed. "If Kinza's with them I'll wake you up to greet her. If not, I shall leave you to find out in the morning."

A little shadow of fear crossed Jenny's face at the possibility of Kinza's not being there. She turned tragic eyes on her mother.

"If Kinza isn't there," she whispered, "I never want to wake up again, never!"

She had so much to think about that she was quite sure she would never go to sleep; and yet, when the light was turned out and she was left alone with the sound of the rushing stream in the valley, her eyes closed almost immediately; and the next thing she knew was that her mother was shaking her gently, and Auntie Rosemary was sitting at the foot of the bed laughing and holding a bundle wrapped up in the car rug in her arms.

"It's Kinza!" cried Jenny, flinging herself on the bundle, and a tremendous hugging and kissing ensued. Kinza opened bright, drowsy eyes, but closed them again in a minute or two, and Jenny, very pink and warm with joy and deep sleep, nestled her head against her aunt's shoulder and heard all about it in a whisper; for after all it was two o'clock in the morning, and there were other guests in the hotel.

Everyone was hungry, so they lit the picnic stove and made tea. Mr. Swift, who was feeling enormously pleased at the success of the expedition, balanced himself on the end of the bed and stirred his sugar with a tooth-brush handle while his wife spread butter and honey on the bread and passed round the biscuits. Never had there been a happier midnight feast, and Jenny was going to remember that hour all her life. Kinza had been brought back, and all her naughtiness and its terrible consequences were forgiven and forgotten. She was going to start again, a new child in a new happy life and, sitting there in

bed with all the people she loved best grouped round
her, and her mouth full of bread and honey, she felt
as full of happiness as the buttercups had been full
of light. Her pure joy infected them all, and although
her mother said rather weakly four times over that
they really must all go to bed, no one took the slightest notice; they just went on eating and whispering.
When Mr. Swift told them how they had escaped
from Si Mohamed, he fell backward in his excitement,
and they all nearly burst with repressed laughter;
whereupon Kinza awoke, and sat up tousled and
majestic, blinking at them solemnly like a baby owl.
She apparently disapproved of all this midnight merriment, for after a few moments she cuddled back
into the depths of the blanket and went to sleep again.
Then Mrs. Swift said for the fifth time that they really
must go to bed and Mr. Swift said, "All right, but
let me just have one more piece because falling off
the bed made me hungry again." Then Auntie Rosemary wanted another piece, and so did Jenny, and
her mother thought she might as well have one too.

Then Mrs. Swift said for the sixth time that they
really must go to bed, and this time they *did* listen to
her. They all kissed Jenny good night and tucked her
up in turn, and then went off down the passage laughing at Mr. Swift, who was trying to walk quietly in
his enormous squeaky shoes, like an elephant trying
to walk on tiptoe. And Jenny was left alone with her
happiness in the dark.

God had heard their prayers and Kinza had come back. She could lie down in peace and sleep, with the white moonlight streaming in on her. She pillowed her cheek on her hand, her thoughts strayed back over the day that lay behind her and she remembered the buttercups. They would all be tight closed now, the curled sepals holding them fast, guarding the golden hearts. They were sealed to all but the touch of light, and perhaps that was why they were so radiant.

Everyone slept on next morning till the sun was high—except Hamid and Aunt Rosemary. They got up at the usual time, Hamid because he had slept excellently all night on the back seat of Mr. Swift's car, and the English nurse because she had a busy day ahead of her. It was still quite early when she was disturbed by loud knocking, and she got up with a little sigh, wishing she could train the Moors once and for all not to come for 2:30 p.m. dispensary at 7:30 in the morning. But when she opened the door she found only Hamid, his hands and face pink and shining from a ducking under the fountain, come to visit her.

His rags were dreadfully torn and dirty, and he had nasty sores on his legs, but the child himself was as eager and brimming with young life as the spring morning. He kissed the nurse's hand, chuckled, and hopped uninvited over the threshold. He seemed to have some particular purpose in his visit, for he stood on one leg and scratched his head for half a minute or so. Then, apparently not feeling quite ready to come to the point, he inquired for Kinza.

"She's all right," said the nurse. "Do you want to come and see her?"

For an answer he skipped upstairs ahead of her to where Kinza lay in her old corner on the mat, her dark head pillowed on her arm, fast asleep. Hamid nodded, well pleased, and then looked round hopefully to see if there was any prospect of something to eat. He had timed his visit perfectly, for the English nurse was just in the middle of her breakfast at the other end of the room. Hamid sat down cross-legged on the floor at a polite distance from the table, his eyes bright with expectation. He had not eaten honey sandwiches in the night, and he was very hungry.

The nurse gave him a bowl of sweet coffee and a big hunk of bread. He sipped it noisily, chuckling with pleasure between the mouthfuls. When he had finished and cleaned out the bowl with his finger for fear of wasting any sugar he drew a little nearer and said confidently, "Teach me to read."

The nurse looked at him doubtfully. "But so many people want to learn to read and they only keep it up about a fortnight. Then my time is all wasted."

He shook his head very emphatically. "I would go on every day, until harvest time," he said, "because then I am going home. My father will be glad to see me at harvest because he's so busy. Could I learn to read before harvest?"

"I should think so," said the nurse, "if you really come every day." Her mind ran over the busy hours and she wondered rather vaguely when she was going to fit in this new demand. But the child seemed very much in earnest.

"Why do you want to learn to read, Hamid?" she asked.

He lifted a sober brown face to hers and told her his simple little story.

"I want to go home," he said. "But if I go home and I can't read, who will go on teaching me the way to Heaven?"

"Then you believe it really is the way to Heaven?"

"Yes; I had a dream. I saw the Lord Jesus with His arms stretched out. I think He was on a cross. And behind the cross was a door, wide open, and He told me it was the way to God. And He told me I was to come to you because it was all written down in your Book."

"Very well," said the nurse quietly. "You can come every day just about now. We'll start at once."

She fetched her book of Arabic letters and found him a very quick pupil. By the end of half an hour he had learned quite a number of letters and was unusually pleased with himself.

"Aa—d—dd—rr—z," he chanted proudly. "Now I can read!"

He skipped off with his head held high, and the nurse went back with a happy heart to clear the breakfast things. She had worked in the town for years, and scores of homeless waifs had heard, through her lips, the way to Heaven. But this little boy had apparently understood, and by way of the Cross he had entered through the wide-open door that led to the shelter of the heart of God.

CHAPTER TWENTY

It Happened on a Hillside

THE VISIT was drawing very near to its close now,
and on the last Saturday they started off early in
the morning and went for a picnic far up in the mountains—Mummy, Daddy, Aunt Rosemary, Jenny, Kinza
and a fat picnic basket, all packed into the car together.

They drove up and up past clustered thatched villages and rocky slopes of heather; they looked down far below them into green gorges, and beyond rose mountains capped with snow. Still on and up sped the car until the road plunged into the cool shadow of pine woods, where round the roots of the giant trees grew real English primroses. They stopped the car, and Aunt Rosemary, who had not seen an English spring for ten years, was up the bank before Jenny, burying her face in the pale flowers.

Cold and clear is the air at that height, strong with the scent of rising pine sap, pure with the breath of snow. Everyone fell silent and breathed deeply. Jenny flitted from clump to clump picking flowers, and having collected all she could hold she sat down on a stump in a patch of sunlight to arrange them. She thought she had never been in such a beautiful forest before, with its drifts of primroses and its checkered green lawns with light and shade and starred with pale purple crocuses. Not far away she could hear the rushing of water and knew that the melted snow was tumbling to the valley, watering the earth and making the sap rise. She stopped arranging her flowers and just sat looking at them. How frail and beautiful they were! They were not so sturdy and merry as the buttercups, but then the buttercups had not lain silent for four months under the weight of snow. Yet they were all alike in that they opened wide to the touch of light, flinging back their petals and lifting adoring faces. Jenny had known what it felt like sitting on the hillside three afternoons before.

And now she wanted to tell Aunt Rosemary about it. She must try to tell her today because there might not be another chance, but she did not know how to begin or how to say it, and she had not the slightest idea how to explain what had happened. Only she had felt quite sure something *had* happened and she must know what was going to happen next. Aunt Rosemary could tell her. "O God," she breathed into the sparkling air, "make Auntie come and talk to me here, so I can tell her!"

And God heard her prayer, for a few minutes later Aunt Rosemary wandered away from the others and came over to Jenny and sat down on the tree-stump beside her.

But although it was such a wonderful chance to tell her, sitting there in the still forest, Jenny could find no words to begin. If only Aunt Rosemary would talk about it first, but Aunt Rosemary didn't; she was talking about English woods hundreds of miles away, dozens of years ago, and Jenny was not the least bit interested. There was only one thing that mattered now, and that was the great big thing that had happened to her two days before; and the more she tried to put it into words the more she found herself wondering what really had happened, and whether anything had happened at all. Perhaps it was all just a particularly bright pretend, and the joy would pass and the light would fade. Her eyes suddenly filled with tears of pent-up longing and then her mother called them to come and have dinner. The chance was gone and perhaps there would not be another one. God had apparently not heard her prayer.

She cheered up at dinner, because the high air had made her so hungry, and after dinner she and her father explored, which was great fun, but all the time there was the pain of disappointment deep down in her heart. Doubt had crept in, and all the light and happiness had gone.

They drove home in the golden evening, Jenny's head leaning against her father's shoulder, and the window wide open to let in the wind. It was a sweet warm wind, scented with arnica, and it made Jenny feel sleepy. She watched the flying landscape through half-closed eyes, until they came to a low water-meadow with white jonquils growing in clumps among the rushes. Then she suddenly remembered that the next day would be Easter Sunday, and she sat up rather quickly.

Jenny liked Easter Sunday. There were always white lilies and narcissi in the breakfast table, and big colored Easter eggs round her plate. She always wore a new white frock and white ribbon in her hair. After breakfast she and her father and mother all went to church, which was unusual and exciting, and as far as Jenny could remember the park was always full of sunshine and bluebells and the orchard full of white blossom. The church too was arrayed in white—

a beautiful riot of blossom, lilies of the valley, narcissi and golden daffodils—and the choir boys in white robes sang "Jesus Christ is risen today . . . Alleluia!"

Here they would not go to church because there wasn't one to go to, but suppose Jenny went to visit Auntie Rosemary early with white flowers—perhaps they could sort of play church together. And talking about churches might make Auntie Rosemary talk about God again, and then perhaps it would be easier to tell. She laid her hand on her father's arm. "Stop, Daddy," she said.

Mr. Swift stopped. "What's up?" he inquired good-naturedly.

"I want to get something," explained Jenny. She jumped out of the car and ran backward a little so that Auntie Rosemary could not see what she was doing. She sped across the field, gathered an armful from the water's edge, wrapped them in her cardigan and sped back to the car. She tumbled in breathless.

"What have you got there, Jenny?" asked her father.

"A secret," replied Jenny. "We can go on now!" Mrs. Swift, who had been watching her nimble little daughter through the back window, smiled and said nothing. It was not till Jenny was tucked in bed and the narcissi were up to their necks in the water-jug that she understood what it was all about.

"Mummy," said Jenny, "it's Easter Sunday tomorrow, and on Easter Sunday there are always white flowers. Can I get up very early and take my narcissi to Aunt Rosemary as an Easter surprise?"

"Why, yes," answered her mother; "I think it would be lovely. She has been so kind to you, Jenny. You can go when you wake up. We won't wait breakfast, as you'll probably stay and have it with her. I'll put out your Sunday clothes now."

She laid out Jenny's best frock and clean white socks, kissed her good night and left her, and Jenny went to sleep at once, comforted and hopeful. Perhaps it was all going to come right after all.

She woke very early, when the watcher on the mosque cried out the dawn prayer-call, just at the time when in England the bells would start ringing to remind people that Jesus Christ had risen. Jenny lay for a time sniffing the narcissus-laden air, listening to the stream, and watching the silver light of sunrise brighten behind the wall of rock across the valley. Then she jumped out of bed, washed and dressed herself with extreme care because it was Easter, and set off.

No one was awake. On the crumbling walls of the fort the ivy trembled in the dawn wind, and on the worn steps, six hundred years old, some homeless beggar children lay asleep, huddled in their rags, their heads pillowed on their arms. And through this stronghold of poverty and ignorance and spiritual darkness passed one little girl dressed in blue, clean, loved and loving, her arms full of white flowers be-

cause Christ had risen again and brought to light life
and immortality.

She knocked at the door sedately, and Auntie Rosemary, who was up and having her breakfast, appeared at the window, surprised at such an early
caller. Seeing who it was she ran down to open the
door, and Jenny bounded joyfully in and held up her
narcissi.

"White flowers for Easter!" she announced triumphantly. "I picked them yesterday without you seeing
me."

They went upstairs hand in hand to where breakfast was laid on a white cloth, with a bowl of primroses in the middle of the table. They arranged the
narcissi in a vase behind the primroses and sat down
to enjoy themselves.

"It looks like a church at Eastertime, doesn't it?"
remarked Jenny. As she spoke the sun rose behind the
mountain and streamed into the room, blessing them
with warmth and light. Jenny wriggled contentedly
nearer to her aunt and helped herself uninvited to
bread, butter, and jam.

"On Easter Sunday at home," she remarked when
she was quite full, "Mummy and Daddy and I always
go to church. It's a pity there isn't a church here,
isn't it, so we could all go together?"

"Yes," answered her aunt, "I do miss going to
church dreadfully; and yet you know, Jenny, it
doesn't really matter in one way. The chief reason

for going to church is to meet God, and we can meet God anywhere. I meet Him here every day in my room; just now when you came I was reading the Easter story and feeling so happy."

"Will you read it to me if you've finished eating?" asked Jenny eagerly, settling herself very comfortably to listen while Aunt Rosemary read about the woman who wept in the garden at dawn. Jenny imagined a garden full of white cherry blossom and narcissus, white as the wings of the angels who guarded the empty sepulcher. But Jesus had met her and called her by her name, and no doubt at that moment the sun rose over the back of the cave, turning all the flower-petals and dewdrops to silver, while Mary was looking up through shining tears, crying "Master!"

"He met Mary in a garden," said Aunt Rosemary; "and He met some of the disciples in a little room, and He met two others on the road, and He met Peter on the beach. So you see it isn't really necessary to go to a building."

"No," said Jenny simply, lifting a bright face; "that's what I wanted to tell you. The other day . . . the day you went to fetch Kinza . . . I thought He met me, up on the hill where the buttercups grow. I asked Jesus to come and live inside me like the light in the lantern, and stop me being cross and selfish. And I felt so happy and I thought He had come. But yesterday I didn't feel happy any more, and I was afraid perhaps it was all pretend. Do you think He really came, Auntie? because I don't really feel very different."

Aunt Rosemary was silent for a moment. Then she said quietly, "Jenny, how did Mary feel quite sure that Jesus had really come to her?"

"When He said her name," answered Jenny a little ruefully. "It was easy for her. She heard Him and saw Him."

"Yes, I know," said Aunt Rosemary, "but it's really quite easy for us too if only we believe that God speaks the truth. I'm going to show you a text, Jenny, and then I'm going to tell you a story."

"Good," said Jenny who loved stories; and she wriggled close to look over Auntie Rosemary's Bible. They read Isaiah, chapter 43, verse 1.

"For thus saith the Lord . . . Fear not: for I have redeemed thee, I have called thee by thy name; thou art Mine."

"That text reminds me of Kinza the night we went to look for her," said Aunt Rosemary glancing at the little hump in the corner that was Kinza asleep. "She was living with me quite happily, but she was stolen, and taken away from me. I love Kinza very much and I knew she'd be unhappy; so I went after her, and I found her hungry and frightened and wanting me. She didn't know I was there, but I knew she was there, so what did I do?"

"Shouted at her!" said Jenny with sparkling eyes.

She knew this story well and would never tire of hearing it again.

Aunt Rosemary laughed. "Yes, that's right," she said. "But we'll put it a bit differently this time. Let's say I called her by her name. I said 'Kinza'—and what did Kinza do?"

"Bustled out from under her rug in no time," cried Jenny, and she too laughed with delight.

"Yes, she bustled out in no time," repeated Aunt Rosemary. "She was unhappy and frightened and she knew if she came she would be safe and happy, so she didn't stop to ask how or why or if it was really me. She knew it was me by the way I called her by her name, and she came straight into my arms and felt perfectly safe; she knew she could trust her 'Ima,' as she calls me. And that's exactly what happened to you on the hillside, Jenny. You didn't know much about Jesus; you were just miserable and tired of yourself. But Jesus knew all about you and He wanted to make you good and happy. So He called you by your name, and you knew it was He and you came at once and felt perfectly safe."

"Only for two days," answered Jenny cautiously.

"Yes, exactly," agreed Aunt Rosemary; "and that's just what happened to Kinza. She hadn't been in my arms two minutes before her stepfather began talking, and Kinza began to tremble and cry. I was holding her just as close and loved her just as much, but as soon as she heard the voice of the man who had stolen

her and beaten her she began to feel afraid and wonder if it was all right after all. And the minute we
come to Jesus, Satan, our old master, who hates us to
be good and happy, begins to talk very loudly in our
hearts and tells us it's all pretend; and as long as we
listen to him we shall feel afraid and worried. But
our feelings don't really matter very much, because
Jesus doesn't change. He holds us just as close and
loves us just as much whether we worry about it or
whether we don't."

"Oh, I see," said Jenny thoughtfully. "I forgot about
Satan."

"Well, you needn't think much about him yet,"
said Aunt Rosemary. "If you are really one with
Jesus Satan can't touch you any more than that
wicked man could take Kinza out of my arms. He can
only frighten you if you listen to him. Now listen
what happened next. I went up to Si Mohamed and
I took the money out of my pocket and paid him; and
if Kinza had been old enough to understand I'd have
said this: 'Don't be afraid, Kinza, I've redeemed you
—that means bought you back again. I called you to
come to me and you came. No one can take you away
from me now. You're my little girl forever.'

"We really belonged to God, because He made us,
but when we did wrong we wandered away from our
real Master, and Satan said, 'They are mine now.' But
Jesus loved us and wanted us back, and was willing
to pay any price to redeem us, to buy us back again.

The wages of sin is death, and Jesus was willing to pay even those wages because we were so precious to Him. He died on the Cross and paid the price, and now when He calls us and we come He says, 'Don't be afraid. I've paid for you. You'll never belong to anyone else now. You're Mine forever!'

"I couldn't explain about the price to Kinza because she was too little and too sleepy, but I did just whisper, 'Don't be afraid, Kinza; you're my little girl now.' And Kinza did a very sensible thing. She believed me and she stopped being afraid. Although that cruel man was still standing in front of her talking, she just clung to me as close as she could and fell quietly asleep in my arms and slept all the way home. And the only way to stop feeling afraid is simply to believe what Jesus says. He died to pay the price of sin. He rose again so that He could live in the heart of every man and woman and boy and girl who hears His call and comes to Him; and if Satan says, 'It's not true; you're still mine,' just answer, 'Jesus says He's redeemed me; He's called me by my name; I'm His forever; I believe Him and I'm not going to be afraid.' "

Jenny sat quite silent, thinking over what her aunt had said, and fingering the white narcissus petals. The sun streamed warm on her hair and she felt perfectly happy because now she understood what had really happened. Jesus had loved her and died for her and paid for her and called her and made her His own. All she had had to do was simply to come, and you couldn't go far wrong over that. All her life long from that moment onward Mary was going to be her favorite Bible character because they had so much in common. They had both got up early on Easter morning, and amid sunshine and white flowers Jesus had called them by their names and taken away their fears and made them happy.

They talked for quite a while after that, and then Kinza woke up and wanted her breakfast, and Jenny went dancing off through the sunshine to find her father and mother. But Rosemary sat very still watching her curly baby who sat with her face buried in her bowl of milk.

She had felt quite sure for the past few days that it was not safe for Kinza to remain with her any longer. As soon as the stepfather wanted more money he could easily hire false witnesses and claim the child. For the next few years she must be taken somewhere out of his reach, and the obvious place was Jenny's Blind School.

And yet what Auntie Rosemary wanted more than anything else for Kinza was that she should be brought up by someone who would teach her to love the Saviour while she was still tiny, and that was why she had hesitated in accepting Mrs. Swift's kind offer. Now she knew the answer quite clearly. She would ask Jenny to teach Kinza, and pray that the Holy Spirit of God would teach Jenny.

CHAPTER TWENTY-ONE

"I Do Love Him Very Much"

WHEN, AFTER the three grown-ups had shut themselves up and talked for an hour, Jenny was finally told that Kinza was going home with them, she nearly went wild with joy and excitement, and danced about like a crazy little lamb. The thought of having Kinza to look after on the journey did much **to** lessen the sorrow of having to say good-by to Aunt

Rosemary; and after all it was not going to be a very
long good-by, as Aunt Rosemary was due home for
a holiday in the summer, and had promised to come
and stay with them all.

The evening before they left, Jenny took her aunt
and Kinza for a last walk to the place where the buttercups grew, and they sat there together for a little
while watching the sunset.

"Are you sad that Kinza's going away, Auntie?"
asked Jenny suddenly.

"Well, of course I shall miss her dreadfully, but I
feel quite happy about her. You see, what I mind
most of all for Kinza is that she shall learn to know
and love the Lord Jesus while she's still tiny, and now
that you know Him you'll be able to teach her. Of
course, I expect she'll learn something at the Blind
School, but such a wee child needs someone special
all to herself to teach her."

Jenny looked very serious.

"I don't know an awful lot myself," she replied
doubtfully; "who'll teach me, Auntie Rosemary? At
school they don't talk like you do. We mostly learn
the names of kings in Scripture. I suppose I could
go to Sunday school, but we usually all go out in the
car on Sunday afternoon."

"Yes, it does seem difficult," said Aunt Rosemary.
"But it's quite all right, because you've got your
Bible, and you've got the Holy Spirit of Jesus in your
heart to show you what it means. There was a king

called David long ago who wanted to understand the
Bible, so he prayed this prayer: 'Open Thou mine
eyes, that I may behold wondrous things out of Thy
law.' God answered his prayer and whenever he read
the Bible he saw all the way to Heaven mapped out
in it; and he said this:

" 'Thy Word is a lamp unto my feet, and a light
unto my path.'

"If you read it faithfully and regularly every day,
asking the Holy Spirit of Jesus to make you understand, you'll find that He lights up and explains all
the things you find dark and difficult."

"There are such long words in it," said Jenny, still
rather doubtful.

"Not in the gospels," answered Aunt Rosemary.
"Start with those. And I'm sure you'll find Mummy
and Daddy willing to explain hard words if you ask
them. They are interested in everything that interests
you. Have you told them what happened to you and
why you want to read the Bible?"

"No," said Jenny frowning, "I wanted to, but somehow I couldn't explain."

"Well, it would be a very good thing to tell them
in words," said Aunt Rosemary, "but a far more
important thing is to tell them by works. If you have
really put the Lord Jesus in the very middle of your
life, if you obey His voice every day as He speaks to
you in the Bible, He will soon change you very much.
His love will begin to show instead of your selfish-

ness, His patience instead of your bad temper, and His helpfulness instead of your laziness. And directly that begins to happen Mummy and Daddy will know all about it without any telling. But I should try to tell too, because it would be such a lovely thing to share."

"Yes," agreed Jenny frankly. "They'd certainly be pleased if I really got nice and good and never got into rages, and I expect they'd want to know why, too. I should think I'd better show them first, and then they'll believe me when I tell them. Let's go home now, and I'll show them I want to help with the packing."

So they hurried home through the sunset as quickly as they could, Auntie Rosemary carrying Kinza in her arms, warm, heavy and drowsy. When they reached home Kinza was fast asleep and hardly woke up even when she was undressed. The parting held no sadness for her. She had been told she was going on a long journey in the big car with Jenny, and that prospect held nothing but pure delight; so she lay breathing peacefully, seeing, no doubt, in her dreams all the lovely things she would never see on earth, her tiny bundle of possessions and her clean clothes for traveling ready beside her.

Next morning at dawn they all gathered at the hotel door to say good-by. Hamid appeared from some secret haunt of his own to see the last of his little sister. Mr. and Mrs. Swift were busy with porters and

bills; and Aunt Rosemary, while she waited, stood
watching the three children whom she had come to
love more than any other children she knew. They
stood in a little group by the luggage—beautiful,
favored Jenny; ragged Hamid; and blind Kinza. What
widely-separated, lonely pathways lay ahead of
them? Thank God there was a Shepherd who cared
for lonely lambs, and a Light to guide their stumbling
feet. And thank God there was a day coming soon
when children of every kindred and tribe and nation
would stand before the throne of God; and in that
day they would all meet again: Jenny set free from
herself, Hamid set free from his fear, and Kinza seeing
the light—all would rejoice together.

A few moments later they had said good-by and
the car drove off toward the green valley. Jenny's
eyes were full of tears, but Kinza, beating excitedly
on the windows, had not yet realized that her dear
"Ima" was not also inside, and when she did realize
she would no doubt be quickly comforted with something to eat. They swept round the corner, and Rosemary was comforted to find that one of her children,
at least, was still close beside her. Hamid was sniffing,
his grimy knuckles pressed to his eyes, because the
baby for whom he had toiled and sacrificed and risked
everything had been swept away to a new world in
a grand car. One great mission of his young life had
been completely successful, but his little sister would
never need him again. For her the fine clothes, and

big cars, and cookies—for him the deserted market place, the hunger, homelessness and rags.

"Come home and have breakfast," said the nurse at his side.

He brightened up instantly and forgot all his troubles—the thought of hot coffee and bread and butter turned all the world rosy. He skipped along beside her, rubbing his hands delightedly. He had no work today because the master had gone to town, so there was plenty of time and, apart from this invitation, no prospect of anything to eat.

When breakfast was over he had his daily reading lesson. He was getting on very fast and the nurse marveled at him. She had taught all types of children —the sheltered little girls from big houses, the wild waifs from the streets; and it was astonishing how much quicker Hamid was at learning. Waifs' wits and memories were sharpened by the struggle they had to keep alive, and they had trained themselves to look and remember. Hamid in a week had mastered all his letters and knew the repeating exercises by heart; in fact, he was rather unduly puffed up.

"Now I know everything," he remarked, beaming as he struggled through a few three-letter words.

"Oh, no, Hamid; you are only just beginning. You must practice and practice putting the letters into words, and you must come every day if you want to read the Word of God by harvest time."

He nodded confidently.

"By harvest time," he repeated. "Then I shall go back and read the Word of God to my mother. Then she will know the way to Heaven too, and when my stepfather beats her and won't give her enough food the Lord Jesus will make her heart happy."

"Will your stepfather let you read the Word of God to her?"

"Oh, no; he says all books are bad but the Koran. But I shall read it in the granary when my mother is grinding corn and I shall read to my sister Rahma when we tend the goats on the mountain. My father will never know."

"But later on, Hamid, he will have to know, if you are going to follow Jesus faithfully. You will have to tell him and he may beat you. But Jesus suffered a great deal for you because He loved you. If you love Him, you must be willing to suffer a little, too."

He turned thoughtful, troubled eyes on her.

"I do love Him very much," he said wistfully, and rose to go, leaving his friend well content with his answer. He had not boasted, nor made any great profession. He had simply laid claim to the greatest power in the universe—"I love Him," that lonely little boy facing his perilous future had said, and many waters cannot quench love, neither can the floods drown it.

CHAPTER TWENTY-TWO

A Gallant Little Apostle

THE END CAME sooner than the nurse had expected —at the time of the great pilgrimage, when the corn stood breast-high in the fields and the days were hot and parched. Everyone who could possibly do so was traveling out to the shrine of a Moslem saint on top of a high mountain twenty miles to the southwest. Crowds of villagers and tribespeople streamed in

249

from outlying regions, the rich on horseback, the poor on foot. Some had come several days' journey from the far Riff mountains, dressed in bright silk garments and gaudy orange turbans. They all passed through the town to stock up with supplies before going farther. The market looked like a great campground with hosts of tired pilgrims settling on the cobbles for the night. All were enjoying themselves and there was plenty to entertain them. There was the grave-dancer whose body only seemed to move from the waist downward, the pipe-players wailing out their mournful dirges, and best of all, as far as the children were concerned, was the tame monkey, which ran up and down a long stick and bowed himself up and down on top, touching his forehead and doubling himself up like a fakir saying his prayers.

There was so much to see and do that only five little boys turned up to the children's meeting that night. They arrived warm and sunburned, for they had been out on the hillside all day long watching the streams of pilgrims and begging from the rich. They carried the spoils of the wheat fields in their arms; they came in single file, filthy and joyful, like a floral procession of black monkeys, and each laid on the table in turn a bright bunch of poppies, moondaisies, and cornflowers. The smallest was left behind and arrived a few moments later running very fast and trailing poppies all down the street—a funny little urchin with no front teeth and no shirt and an enormous pair of black trousers tied round his waist with a rope.

Then as she stood surveying this joyous company Rosemary noticed something different about them. They were very excited, and each carried a pilgrim staff in one hand and a tattered basket in the other. Their feet were bound up with rough leather strips.

"We are going to the Saint's shrine," they informed her eagerly. "We shall travel all night with the pilgrims because of the heat, and arrive at daybreak. For five days we shall camp near the shrine and see the people, and hear the music and watch the men with the tame monkeys. See, we have collected enough bread for the journey and we are all ready to start at sunset; but there's time for our story and our supper first."

They opened their little baskets proudly, and each displayed a dry collection of old brown crusts and a bottle of water. Hamid's alone held something else besides. He carried his precious New Testament which he had earned the week before when he managed to stumble through the first chapter of St. John's Gospel. He alone seemed sad, and the nurse glanced at him rather anxiously. The boys might look on the whole thing as a sort of summer holiday, but a heathen shrine was no place for a Christian child.

"How long are you going to stay there, Hamid?" she asked.

"I'm not staying there," he replied simply. "I'm going home. I can travel tonight with the pilgrims, and rest tomorrow. Then the next night a lot of them will go to another shrine not far from my village and I can travel with them. I can read now, and the harvest is nearly ripe. If I wait, I shall have to go the long way round by the road, for I could never find my way over the mountains alone. I had better go now."

"Yes, I suppose you had," agreed the nurse slowly, and they gathered round her and she told them of the weeping pilgrims long ago who had visited a sepulcher and found it empty—and how two of them had set out on a long walk at sunset, and the risen Lord Jesus had drawn near and walked with them and gone in to abide with them. Hamid sat very close to her and never took his eyes off her face.

The nurse brought in supper, and they scooped up their lentils in their hands. But they tucked their hunks of bread into their baskets to eat on the road, and leaped to their feet, eager to start. She went to the doorstep with them. The street was bright with sunset. They seemed to be setting out on a golden journey, and they lifted joyful grimy faces to hers as they bade her farewell. She looked down at them, and her heart ached because of the weary, sleepless night ahead, the coldness of the dawn and the dryness of those crusts. She ran back into her kitchen, fetched a dish of cherries and gave them a big handful each; they squeaked and chuckled with pleasure, and, once again, for the last time, she tried to make them understand.

"You are going to see the tomb of a dead man," she said very earnestly, "and we like to remember dead men if they were good and true, but a dead man can't help anyone. The Lord Jesus arose from the dead. He's alive now, loving you, and He'll go with you all the way."

Four heads nodded, for they were impatient to be off, but Hamid drew very close to her and looked up, his face rather pale, but suddenly bright.

"Yes," he replied, "the Lord Jesus is alive. He lives in our hearts and He'll go with us all the way."

The other boys were already scampering down the street, swinging their baskets, their pilgrim staves clattering on the cobbles, the smallest one already spitting out his cherry stones. So she prayed a blessing on Hamid and sent him forth, and he followed them, his face turned back to her, smiling through tears, a lonely little apostle of Jesus Christ. He had much farther to travel than the others, but packed in with the crusts and the water-bottle and the cherries he carried the staff of life and the bread of Heaven, and by night on the rough mountain roads his young feet would not stumble much nor stray far. Jesus said, "I am the Light of the world: he that followeth Me shall not walk in darkness, but shall have the Light of Life."

At the end of the street they all turned and waved, five gay little figures black against the sunset. Then they turned the corner, and the light seemed to swallow them up.

To the young people who have read this book:

Some of you sometimes write and ask whether the stories I write for you are true.

This story is made up of incidents from the lives of children I have known and I have woven them into the life of one child. Jenny is mostly made up, and the nurse might be one of any of the missionaries who work among children in Morocco.

But the story has been written to give you a true picture of what can, and does, happen to children who live in a land where Jesus Christ is unknown. Without Christianity there is often very little kindness and mercy, and no hope or real joy. But if you think this is rather a sad book remember that you may pray and take an interest in those who have gone out to preach the Gospel. You can help to bring light and happiness to these children.

I live in the town to which Hamid brought Kinza, and I have stayed in his home village. I have known many little boys turned out homeless into the street because their mothers married again, and I have heard of unwanted babies left on doorsteps. I have seen blind children hired out to beggars, and known of others, once happily adopted, who have been snatched back into lives of misery. I have also seen many who have traveled long weary miles in search of healing, and sometimes we missionaries have been able to help them.

On the other hand I have known men, women, and little children who were sad and sinful and afraid, and whose lives have been changed by the Gospel. All that Hamid said on the subject has been said to me by a homeless little boy who I believe has found real happiness because he heard about and accepted the Lord Jesus. There could be many more like him but there are so few missionaries to tell them.

So as you think of the town to which Hamid and Kinza traveled and of the long, long valley in which it lies, with its Eastern snow-capped Riff mountains and its hundreds of villages, will you sometimes pray for the children who live there?

Your friend,
PATRICIA ST. JOHN